Oh F*ck it's Christmas

A SURVIVAL GUIDE FOR ANYONE WHO'S EVER WANTED TO SET FIRE TO THE TREE.

KARIE S NYARAI

ACCOUNTABILITY WORKS

Contents

Dedication

THIS ONE'S FOR YOU, MUM — YOU'LL ALWAYS BE THE STAR ON MY TREE.

To my mom,

The original architect of Christmas magic, who managed to make every holiday feel special, even if the mince pies looked suspiciously store-bought.

Thanks for showing me how to create memories that last a lifetime—and for proving that even when everything goes wrong, there's always room a one-liner that deserves its own Christmas card.

You've always been the strongest spirit I know: steadfast, supportive, and ready with the perfect mix of wisdom and wit—often delivered with a side of sarcasm that would make even the Grinch grin.

My mom, my top cheerleader and fiercest protector, showed me love is in the effort—and that even when chaos reigns, the best plan is to laugh, carry on, and make a trifle so good it's almost legendary (wine in hand, of course).

About the author

KARIE S NYARAI

No, Karie S Nyarai isn't her real name. It's a pen name—because the only way to keep the real names of the characters intact was to disguise her own. That way, everyone in her stories knows exactly who they are (without the risk of lawsuits or a family WhatsApp drama).

Born in Zimbabwe and now living in Perth, Western Australia, Karie has successfully raised three beautiful children into fully grown humans old enough to raid her fridge, borrow her car, and then move out so she can squeeze in yet another pet. Fortunately, she also has an amazing partner who never questions her dubious adoption habits. The pets, naturally, have become understudies for the kids' furry replacements who don't argue about curfews or leave their laundry everywhere.

These days, Karie views wrinkles as survival medals: each one an explicit permission slip. They bring wisdom, sass, and that blissful "I don't care" edge. Beneath her crisp exterior, however, she's still as tender as butter abandoned in Perth's blistering sun.

"If survival is the true spirit of life, then I'm basically the patron saint of Christmas chaos, questionable decisions, and showing up anyway—with a glass of wine in hand."
— Karie S. Nyarai

Acknowledgements

To my three wonderful children Nick, Kiffy, and Danni. You are my greatest creations. Nick, thoughtful and calm in chaos, the quiet strength that reminds me how grace can be steady even in a storm. Kiffy, alive with adventure, reminding us that life is meant to be lived out loud, and in full colour. Danni, full of fire, blazing your own trail with a spark no one can dim.

There is nothing in this world I adore, admire, and am prouder of than you three. You are my heart's masterpiece the living, laughing, fiercely brilliant proof that love creates the most extraordinary things.

Courts my "daughter" from another mother, you have shown me how to laugh, till I am crunched over and the tears are rolling down my face.

You are *all* the reason I laugh, cry, and keep buying more wine.

To my amazing friends in Perth, from every corner of the world, who have picked up the pieces more times than I can count—thank you. You've been my tribe, my emergency helpline, my 2 a.m. voice of reason (and occasional bad influence). You've shown up with wine when words failed, humour when hope wobbled, and hugs that stitched me back together. You're the reason I've survived more Christmases (and Mondays) than I thought possible, proof that family isn't always born, sometimes it's beautifully found.

To those who have screwed me over: thank you. Truly. You were the unexpected tutors in my crash course on boundaries, resilience, and the fine art of sarcasm. Without you, I wouldn't have had nearly as much material. You were the gift that kept on giving, wrapped in red flags and tied with the ribbon of life lessons I never asked for but desperately needed.

Finally, to Mark, the most wonderful human being I have ever met. You've shown me what it means to be loved and to feel truly safe. No words can do that justice, but I'll spend the rest of my life trying. You are my calm, my joy, and the reason I finally stopped dreading Christmas quite so much.

Diss - Claimer !!!

BEFORE STARTING THE STORIES, LET ME CLEARLY STATE THIS FESTIVE DISCLAIMER SO YOU KNOW MY PURPOSE FOR INCLUDING IT:

This book is a work of fiction, with stories inspired by real events. Real life writes the best material. My goal here is to entertain, not expose. I'm not about to name names directly. Right? Actually—yes. Yes, I will. Because if you've inspired the story, you've earned your place in it. Consider it my version of a Christmas card, just with slightly more truth and fewer sparkles.

If you happen to see some of your behaviours between these pages, it's purely coincidental... or maybe a gentle nudge from the universe to reflect on your festive behaviour. Either way, relax, it's all in good fun. Mostly.

Before you accuse me of being passive-aggressive: YES, this is absolutely my way of calling things out while still clinging (white-knuckled) to the plausible deniability that fiction so graciously offers. It's my emotional loophole, my literary witness protection program. Think of it as therapy, but cheaper and with better dialogue. Besides, if the shoe fits, darling, consider this your gentle reminder to stop wearing it.

Think of it as a festive mirror, shiny, slightly warped, brutally honest and held up to the chaos, with just enough sparkle to make you laugh while you reflect.

So, grab a cup of tea or wine or whatever tickles your fancy and dive in, and remember, "It's all in good fun".

Unless it isn't.

In that case, may your presents be practical, your baubles remain uncrushed, and your lessons come dusted with a heap of extra glitter (the kind that never leaves, no matter how much you vacuum).

"Christmas isn't ruined by chaos; it's built on it. Anyone who tells you different is lying—or has staff."
— Karie S. Nyarai

Before the Glitter Hits the Fan

Christmas. The season of joy, cheer, and... crushing guilt, barbed family texts, and at least one full-blown meltdown by Boxing Day. You know the modern classics.

If you picked up this book hoping for a wholesome Christmas story, I'm afraid you're about to be as disappointed as I was the year I unwrapped a book on *Emotional Intelligence,* complete with a card that said, "Thought you could use this." *Wow!!!* In hindsight... maybe they had a point.

This is not that kind of wholesome Christmas story.

No, this is the other kind, the brutally honest, wine-fuelled, slightly unhinged version. It's equal parts confession, comedy, and survival manual for anyone who's ever looked at Christmas and thought, there has to be a better way to do this.

Christmas perfection is a scam, and I'm done pretending that it is "the most wonderful time of the year".

I want you to know that if you have ever fantasised about setting fire to the tree or re-gifting a present to the person who gave it to you last year, you are not alone.

This is your permission slip to drop the act, lower the bar low enough even a weasel couldn't limbo under it—and reclaim a Christmas that doesn't require a therapy session come January.

This isn't a book about hating Christmas. It's a book about reclaiming it—glitter, chaos, and all.

It's about letting go of the unnecessary, rethinking joy, and breaking free from the societal pressures that bind us to the illusion of perfection.

It's about laughing at the chaos, finding humour in the absurdity, and discovering what really matters.

Here's the plan: I'll overshare my disasters faster than Santa's elves clocking off at midnight. You'll laugh (or wince in recognition), and along the way, you'll get unapologetic permission to do less and ditch the guilt.

Because let's be honest, when you hit fifty and the kids have flown the nest, you stop giving a single festive fuck about keeping up appearances. If it doesn't spark joy or at least pour you a nice cold drink, it should be dead to you. True story.

So, pour yourself something strong—wine, whiskey, or electrolytes if you're feeling delicate and let's get this party started.

Let's also give a hearty FU to Christmas and all its glitter-covered nonsense and embrace the chaos as that is where the magic lives.

Merry chaos,

Karie

Official Permission

TO PAUSE, REFLECT, LAUGH, AND LET GO

By the **highly questionable authority** vested in me as the author of *OH F*ck it's Christmas,* I hereby grant:

_____ **(Your Name Here)**

Permission to:

Pause. Take a breath, step back, and let the chaos swirl around you like tinsel in a wind tunnel—without a shred of guilt.

Reflect. Remember what actually matters.

Laugh. At the absurdity, the imperfections, and that one relative who still can't figure out how to turn their camera on during a WhatsApp call.

Let Go. Of guilt and unrealistic expectations.

Signed,

Karie S Nyarai
Certified Chaos Survivor & Defender of Crooked Christmas Trees

Acceptance of Permission Slip

I, _____ **(Your Name Here),** whole-heartedly accept this Permission Slip to Pause, Reflect, Laugh, and Let Go during the holiday season embracing one gloriously imperfect moment at a time!

Date: _____ **(The first day of the rest of your sanity)**

How to Use This Book

(Without Needing Therapy After)

Inside, you'll find a balancing act: part deep emotional insight, part get-your-shit-together empowerment. At the end of each chapter, you'll find two little gems and a Quote.

1- Exercises to Complete

These are reflective, sometimes funny, sometimes rip-your-heart-open writing prompts intended to help you unpack your own festive baggage. It's your chance to call things out as what they are, make peace with the mess, and take the opportunity to rewrite a few of your holiday rules. They are your invitation to make this season yours and work out what matters most to you and your family, rather than running with expectations of Christmas's gone or demanding relatives.

2 - Take 5 – Checklist

Quick, practical, doable actions you can take right now. These are your tiny rebellions against guilt, perfectionism, and that one relative who still thinks asking about your love life is "small talk." There will be no journaling required on these. They are just five fierce, fabulous steps served with a wink and the ability for you to do them with a glass of your favourite vino.

Do one.

Do them all.

Start a support group or just read and nod along while drinking wine in the pantry.

No pressure—this isn't school.

No judgment.

No rules.

CHAPTER ONE

The Most Wonderful Time of the Year - thanks Andy Williams

W hen I was ten, I learned that Christmas was a common time for people to commit suicide. I remember thinking: *Why Christmas? Isn't it just another day? Surely everyone has someone to be with?*

Nearly thirty years later, on Christmas Day, I understood.

It was 2013. Christmas Day. Toodyay, Western Australia. Instead of the warm messy joy of a Zimbabwean holiday surrounded by family, long term friends and tradition, I was alone on a farm. Alone. Me, cows and my veggies. I'd imagined rural life would give my kids freedom to run wild in the wide skies, come home with dirty knees, and be free – a childhood like mine had been.

It was like that most of the time but on that Christmas day that "freedom" boomeranged.

The kids were in Perth with their dad. The house was quiet, too quiet, the kind of silence that presses against you until you can hear your own heartbeat. I wandered from room to room like a ghost in my own life, the wrapping paper still on the floor, the fridge full of leftovers no one would eat, and not a soul to share it with.

Christmas Day, and it was just me.

Eventually, I did what any emotionally stable woman would do, I escaped to the veggie patch. Out there, I could finally let it all spill without having to pretend. No brave face, no forced smiles, just me, the sun, and the quiet honesty that comes when no one's around to see you fall apart. So, hose in hand, I started watering the lettuces and zucchinis—though, let's be honest, probably more with tears than water...

Somewhere in the background, Andy Williams was bellowing *It's the Most Wonderful Time of the Year*, while I was ugly-crying into zucchini plants. Get real, Andy. Wonderful for who? The people ice-skating past department store windows in your snow globe? Out here the only "snow" I can see is the dust from the neighbour's ute, and the closest thing I had to chestnuts roasting on an open fire was a tragically burnt sausage on the barbie.

Somewhere between the tomatoes and the rosemary it hit me: this was the kind of Christmas my ten-year-old self could never have imagined. No chaos, no clinking glasses, no familiar noise. Just me, my vegetables, and the low buzz of flies playing carols in B-flat. It was dreadful.

The sun was merciless, branding me like it had a personal vendetta against me. Poetic, really, scorched outside, burning inside. My naïve belief in automatic Christmas joy collapsed like a deck of cards. I'd crossed the line from thinking Christmas was magic by default to knowing it could just as easily be something you endure.

It wasn't that I had *no one*. It was that the people I wanted the most weren't there. They were scattered all around the world, or in Perth living their other life.

Staring at the zucchini plants, I realised they were thriving far more than my social life and, frankly, looking a lot less desperate for attention. Their leaves were lush, their blossoms wide open to the world, while I stood there feeling like an overwatered houseplant left too long in the shade.

That's when it hit me: I finally understood how Christmas could be the loneliest day of the year. It's not the silence itself that hurts, it's the contrast. The world hums with forced joy, neighbours laugh over fences, the radio won't shut up about togetherness, and there you are standing in the dirt, trying to remember the last time someone looked at you the way you look at your zucchinis, with quiet admiration and a hint of pride.

Until then, loneliness had been rare. Back in Zimbabwe, Christmas meant connection: people dropping by unannounced, the smell of food wafting through open windows, friendships with roots deeper than baobabs. That year, Christmas on the farm was my first taste of loneliness that you can point to and name: empty chairs, silence pressing in, and the absence of the faces you love most.

In the years to come, I would discover something even more brutal than loneliness: invisibility. Loneliness stings, but invisibility convinces you you're not even worth unwrapping.

Being alone, I could handle it. You fill the silence, make peace with your own company, invent small rituals. Being unseen? That's a wound all its own.

I didn't know it then, but that quiet Christmas in Toodyay was the first loose thread in my ugly festive jumper and once you start pulling, you can't stop. Before long, the whole thing unravels in your hands. But it wasn't all bad. What came undone wasn't the magic; it was the illusion. I started to see Christmas for what it really was a high-pressure pantomime wrapped in tinsel, where joy feels rehearsed, effort goes unnoticed, and no matter how hard you try, there's never a standing ovation for burning yourself out in the name of holiday spirit.

The disillusionment was like a party popper exploding in slow motion: first the shock and the mess, then the confetti. Small, surprising, and somehow exactly what I needed. **Out of the wreckage came a gift I didn't expect**: the realisation that I could take Christmas back. Strip it down. Make it mine again.

No soundtrack.

No snow globe - sorry, Andy Williams.

Just me and the raw, unwrapped version of the day.

Tinsel in the bin, impossible expectations cremated, and the only thing sparkling, well that would be the wine in my glass. Hallelujah for that.

Maybe "The most wonderful time of the Year" isn't December 25th at all. Maybe it's whenever you stop giving a festive hoot about other people's rules and start playing by your own.

Don't worry — I know that was heavy. This ride isn't all zucchinis and tears.

Things are about to get fun, so buckle up we're hitching Rudolph to this emotional sleigh and taking him for a joyride while throwing out all our "Christmas Baggage" from the sleigh. There will be detours, chaos, and probably the occasional crash into a tinsel-covered fence, but I promise you this: it's going to be one hell of a ride.

Lesson: *The Most Wonderful Time of the Year – thanks Andy Williams*

Loneliness isn't just being alone—it's realising the people who matter most aren't there... and haven't been for a while. It's the moment when the fantasy collapses and Christmas jingles mock you from a cracked speaker. But buried under the dust and disappointment is a stubborn truth: Christmas doesn't have to look magical to feel meaningful. Sometimes it's in the unraveling that we finally get to rebuild it, quietly, honestly, and entirely on our own terms.

Exercises to Complete

- **The "Absolutely" Crew**
  These are your ride-or-die, hold-your-hair-back, text-you-at-2 a.m. people. Write down three names, the ones who always show up for you. If you only have one name that is also ok. Then send them a message right now: *"You're my kind of Christmas magic."* Cheesy? Yes. Powerful? Absolutely.

- **The Ghost-of-Christmas-Past Group**
  Exes. Flaky friends. Energy vampires. The people who think your emotional bandwidth is an all-you-can-eat buffet. Write their names down.

Next to each, scrawl: *"Access denied. No more festive freebies."* Then pick your weapon of choice: delete their number, mute or unfollow, leave them on read, or for dramatic flair—burn the paper to the soundtrack of Gloria Gaynor's "I will Survive."

- **What the Hell Happened to Christmas?**
Make a brutally honest list of things you *used* to love about Christmas—and what's changed. Be petty. Be dramatic. Get it all out. Then, pick one thing from the "used to love" list and intentionally bring it back this year. Even if it's just for you. Especially if it's just for you.

- **Make a "You-First" Wishlist**
Forget everyone else's wish lists. What's on yours? A nap? A laugh? A bubble bath? A total absence of small talk? Write down five things that would make this season joyful *for you*. Pick one and actually do it. No guilt. Zero apologies.

Take 5 – Checklist

- **Unmute Yourself**
Speak up once this season when you normally wouldn't. Say no. Ask for help. Correct someone when they assume you're "fine."

- **Find One Thing That Feels Like Home**
Whether it's a song, a scent, or a memory—reconnect with something that grounds you in warmth.

- **Notice the Quiet One**
Be the person who sees someone else's loneliness. Offer a chair, a smile, or the sacred words: *"How are you really?"*

- **Create a New Connection Ritual**
Whether it's a solo champagne toast, a Zoom call with your chosen

family, or a silent night walk—mark the season with a ritual that belongs only to you.

- **Burn the Illusion**
  Write down one expectation, role, or obligation that's sucking the joy out of Christmas. Rip it up. Torch it. Bonus points if you cackle while it burns.

Quote of Choice:

"The worst kind of loneliness is being with people who make you feel alone." – **Robin Williams**

(Because sometimes the bravest gift you can give yourself is walking out of the room where you're invisible—and into the one where you finally shine.)

CHAPTER TWO

Glitter and Guilt

C hristmas had become a battleground, a yearly test of endurance—not just for my patience but for my self-worth. Nobody officially declared war, but there I was drafted, armed with tinsel and a dangerous amount of passive-aggression, determined to win. To be honest, I wasn't entirely sure anyone else was playing.

Why do we do this to ourselves? Why do we sign up for these unspoken Christmas Comparison Wars where the only prize is exhaustion? We convince ourselves that if everything is "perfect," it somehow proves we're winning at life. We're not. We're just really, really tired.

In my world, Christmas wasn't a holiday, it was a mental battleground, and I was the reluctant soldier armed with wrapping paper. My main rival? My ex, of course. The man's house perpetually smelled of cedarwood and smug satisfaction, like a cologne called "Emotional Superiority." His tree stood there, a monument to overachievement, designer-perfect, symmetrical enough to make an architect weep, and tall enough to have been helicoptered directly from the Crown Casino lobby. Every branch was curated, not decorated, each bauble strategically placed to reflect just the right amount of light in that years colour them.

Meanwhile, back at my place, the theme was "survival." The tree leaned like it had hit the eggnog too early. The ornaments? A chaotic mix of sentimental hand-me-downs and glitter-encrusted monstrosities the kids had made at school that year (and which I was morally obligated to hang while loudly declaring, *"Awesome! my Darling"*). The napkins? Paper, with Santa winking like he knew damn well I was winging it.

Yet, as always, the reports from Dad's house rolled in, delivered by children as wide-eyed as if they'd just won lifetime passes to Wet'n'Wild. "Dad had a cheese board with twelve cheeses!" they said, as though I'd been depriving them of camembert all these years. "And there was a chocolate fountain!"

A fountain.

Of chocolate. O.F.F.S. (if you are not sure what that means...look it up!).

It wasn't just the food. At his place, the kids unwrapped a mountain of glossy, expensive presents straight out of Santa's luxury catalogue (I think Santa had a Black Amex and a personal shopper). The wrapping alone at his place probably cost more than the secondhand treasures I'd scavenged from Cash Converters, each one chosen with ridiculous care and the kind of stubborn optimism only a mother on a budget can muster.

I imagined them seeing the thought behind each gift, the hours I'd spent hunting through dusty shelves and tangled cords, searching for something that felt right. I imagined them recognising the love tucked inside every imperfect find, understanding that this was more than a present, it was proof I'd paid attention, that I knew who they were and what might make them smile. In my head, they'd unwrap meaning.

They didn't. But at least the Cash Converters lady appreciated my effort. They tore through them in three seconds flat, leaving me with shredded paper, deflated hope, and the lingering thought that maybe I should've left the price tags on just for emphasis.

Then there was... her. The girlfriend. Perfect, polished, and permanently glowing. She was the kind of woman whose *effortless* existence made you wonder if she had an actual job or just floated from yoga to candlelight dinners in slow motion. But yes... the job. Of course she wasn't just beautiful, she was *accomplished*. A high performer, the kind of woman who somehow manages to climb the career ladder in heels without breaking a sweat or a nail. The LinkedIn type. You know, the one whose bio reads something like: *"Driven. Passionate. Making an impact."* and somehow, she is.

You just knew she'd been the one to assemble the charcuterie board with twelve cheeses, probably while decorating the tree, solving world hunger, and baking gluten-free reindeer cookies in a mess free apron that reads *Baking Spirits Bright*.

Yet, not even a hair out of place.

Meanwhile, I had spent two sticky, chocolate-splattered days crafting the chocolate-dipped oranges of my childhood. Two days. Forty-eight hours where my kitchen looked nothing like Nigella's Christmas special had promised. There were pots sticky with sugar, spoons welded together with burnt caramel, orange peels strewn about, and me, standing in the middle of it all looking dazed and confused.

Nothing about it was graceful.

My apron was streaked with chocolate handprints. The dog had a mysterious smear across its rear, and my hair had clearly joined in the festivities while my cheek was caked with chocolate.

How could I compete with that? She was power suits and Pilates; I was track pants and trauma recovery.

It wasn't that I didn't like her. I just didn't like how much she reminded me of everything I wasn't, calm, curated, and effortlessly together. Standing next to her, I felt like the human equivalent of a tangled box of Christmas lights, functional, but only after a lot of swearing and several glasses of wine.

But these oranges weren't just candy, they were tradition. Nostalgia. A secret handshake with my mum and Auntie Peggy. Proof that some kinds of magic couldn't be bought, no matter how shiny the wrapping paper. I had to get them done.

Trying to keep up with the ex-wasn't just expensive, it was exhausting. I glazed, baked, and carved it like I was auditioning for MasterChef. Yes, that was me, no store-bought rubbish I was going to do it all myself. All this for Christmas Eve, my "fake Christmas." The consolation prize for parents without custody on the real day. The participation ribbon for the main Christmas event before you send them off to their other Christmas, where there will be shinier presents, more people, and a girlfriend who never has chocolate smudged on her elbows.

Every choice is a performance, every detail a silent plea: *See? I'm enough.*

Christmas can easily become a scoreboard. Who gave the flashiest gifts? Who had the better ham glaze? Whose Instagram sparkled the brightest? If you fall short? Well, better start stockpiling tinsel for next year's comeback attempt.

That's the danger of the illusion. On the surface it's all glitter and harmony; behind the scenes it's sweat, swearing, and the gnawing ache of being *less than.*

The truth is, the race is unwinnable. It was never about him, or her, or the kids. It was about me trying to prove to *myself* that I still mattered.

That I was still worthy.

But somewhere in the chaos, the joy got buried under receipts, wrapping paper, and silent comparisons.

So, tap out. Put down the battle plans. End the "Glazed Ham War".

In the end all the fussing, all the comparing, all the frantic effort to keep up with other people's Christmas perfection, it never mattered. The kids don't remember which house had the prettier napkins or who served the brie with artisanal crackers versus stale Jatz. They remember the laughter, the noise, the fact that someone cared enough to try.

If the tree topples, call it a new tradition. If the presents are wrapped in recycled paper bags with "Woolworths" still printed on them, then congratulations, we just invented eco-chic.

I'm done chasing someone else's idea of Christmas. Mine is messy, noisy, sticky with chocolate, and punctuated with eyerolls and inappropriate jokes and I wouldn't swap for anything. This year I's embracing it my way. I'll be laughing at the chaos, eating chocolate oranges straight off the tray, and sipping wine out of my $4 Salvos mug that proudly declares *World's Okayest Mum*.

And you know what? I am and that is enough.

Lesson: *Glitter and Guilt*

Christmas isn't a competition—not with your ex, not with your Instagram feed, and not with the smug overachievers who can "casually" whip up a three-tier grazing table. The exhausting, emotional Olympics of trying to "keep up" will never end well. Your worth isn't measured by how symmetrical your tree is, how many cheeses you served, or whether your gifts came from Salvos or a David Jones.

It's measured in love, thoughtfulness, and maybe the occasional Pinterest fail that at least made someone laugh.

Exercises to Complete

- **Glitter Audit**

    Look back at last year. Which things did you do for show? Was it the perfect bows, extra tinsel, themed desserts nobody touched? Circle the ones that drained you. Cross them off this year's to-do list. Replace them with something that will make *you* smile.

- **The "Not a Scoreboard" List**
  Write down all the sneaky ways you've turned Christmas into a competition: the matching outfits, the gift mountain, the Pinterest-worthy grazing platters. Next to each, note why you did it. Was it for you or for the audience? Then pick one and let it go this year. No scoring, no comparing, no applause required.

- **Fake Christmas Redemption**
  If you've ever hosted the "other" Christmas, you know, Christmas Eve, Boxing Day, or any day that wasn't the main event—jot down three ways to make that day unapologetically yours.

Take 5 – Checklist

- **Reframe a Fail**
  Pick one thing that didn't go perfectly last year and flip it into a win. ("The turkey was dry, but so was the wine, and everyone still laughed.")

- **Let the Tree Lean**
  Leave something imperfect on purpose this year. The tree. The napkins. Your eyeliner. Let it lean. Let it live.

- **Let Tinsel Be Tinsel**
  Tinsel is tacky by design. So is Christmas. So is life. Let something be gloriously over-the-top and shamelessly wrong.

- **Declare a Truce**
  Stop comparing your Christmas to anyone else's, yes, even the ex's. Call a mental ceasefire and keep your eyes on your own joy.

- **Cut the Copycat Cord**
  If you find yourself imitating someone else's Christmas idea, pause and ask: *Would I still do this if no one saw it?*

Quote of Choice:

"It's not how much we give but how much love we put into giving." — **Mother Teresa**

(And honestly, she never once had to compete with a chocolate fountain.)

CHAPTER THREE

The Power of Tinsel and Orange Peels

C hristmas time during my childhood was not a spectacle; it was a feeling. There was always familiar laughter drifting through the house, the clink of mismatched glasses, and the quiet comfort of knowing you belonged.

It was helping Mum in the kitchen, setting the table together and sneaking a treat before anyone noticed, while Dad did his part behind the bar making sure everyone was well "watered".

In the '70s and '80s, catalogues didn't dictate our desires. We saw the glossy South African catalogues, full of shiny promises and "must-have" toys, but they were fantasy, not for us Zimbo kids.

Those things were not for sale where we lived. Shopping wasn't a quick errand; it was a huge event, only possible if you traveled across the border to South Africa an approximate 12-hour trip. (That was after the war finished. Before that it was convoy all the way, a full day to do half the trip to just the border).

Until then, you made do with what you had. In a strange way, it was freeing without a barrage of things to crave, you weren't consumed by the urge to have.

If you wanted something, you made it. If you couldn't make it, you got creative.

One year, Mum and Auntie Peggy decided all our gifts would cost under $10. Auntie Peggy made chocolate-dipped candied orange peels, packed in old coffee jars she'd rescued from the pantry.

Those chocolate oranges were proof with a bit of creativity and love, you could create one the best Christmas presents I have ever received.

Decades later, when I think of Christmas, I remember those jars of orange peels. I don't remember the things I never had, the things that we could not get from those glossy catalogues.

It was an innocent time, before I learned about the "Tinsel Boa Constrictor" shiny, cheerful, and slowly squeezing the joy out of you.

Tinsel doesn't look dangerous. At first glance, it looks harmless even charming. You toss a strand on the tree and think, *Oh, this will make things festive.* But it multiplies. One strand becomes three, three become ten, and suddenly you've got a full-on glitter snake coiled around your neck, whispering: *More lights. A bigger ham. Hand-stencilled napkin rings.*

Soon you'll find you can't breathe. The Boa doesn't let go easily it squeezes tighter with every "*just one more thing*" you think you must have.

That's the problem with Christmas expectations, they slither in innocently, just a little sparkle, here and there until they're dictating every move you make. Suddenly you're knee-deep in ribbon, re-baking gingerbread men because the first batch's buttons weren't evenly spaced and panic-buying fairy lights because your neighbour's display makes yours look like an afterthought. You forget what the day is even for because you're too busy staging it to look like joy instead of actually feeling joy.

When I first had my own family, the "Tinsel Boa Constrictor" hadn't slithered into view yet. I can still picture the kids, their chubby little bums darting in and out of the pool, shrieking with delight, the sun beating down while the day stretched ahead unhurried and uncomplicated.

It wasn't about impressing anyone. It was about being together in all our messy, beautiful imperfection. Where no-one cares when the ZESA (power) goes out and you have to finish the ham on the braai (barbeque) because there's no other choice.

Or laughing at the lopsided paper hat on Dad's head as he told another "Questionably appropriate" joke and raised his glass for another toast to all of us sitting around the table. All this to the background noise of the the gleeful shrieks of the kids cannonballing into the pool for the hundredth time. It was simple, it was peaceful, it was joyful.

Moving to Australia flipped my confidence on its head especially when it came to Christmas parenting. Suddenly my barefoot Christmases with kids running wild did not seem like it was enough. It was so "Third World", so not "Modern First World". It felt like every other parent had been issued a glossy handbook titled *How to Raise Children in the First World at Christmas,* and my copy had gone missing in the mail.

That's when "The Tinsel Boa" really made its move wrapping tighter with every comparison I made, squeezing harder until the air felt thin.

At first it was matching pyjamas, colour-coordinated wrapping paper, the kind of "casual" cheese board that required a degree in architecture. But with each little choice "The Boa" tightened its grip. One photo here, one comparison there, and suddenly I wasn't celebrating Christmas I was auditioning for it.

The strangle was slow to start; it squeezed slowly, with every scroll, every side-by-side mental tally it got tighter. The tighter the squeeze the more frantic my struggle became. By the time I realised, the joy had been wrung out of the season like the last drop of wine from a cheap cask.

Over the years, I tried to wriggle free from "The Tinsel Boa" and resurrect some of that good old Third World magic. The kind built on imagination, scraps, and a low budget. So, while my neighbours were queuing at Myer for the latest "must-have" toy, I was busy at Salvos.

I was being *resourceful*... though, yes, my kids still call it "Mum being stingy in a Santa hat."

One year, we drew names from a hat with one rule: all gifts had to come from Salvos (my favourite "designer" label) or the Tip Shop. Move over Gucci—here comes Good Sammy. Honestly, it was next-level joy, and it still brings us joy today, not for the gifts (let's be honest), but for the sheer drama it unleashed (and yes, more on that chaos shortly).

There's a thrill in wandering those thrift shop aisles, digging through the junk to find something "just right" for your loved one. It forces you to think: *What would make them laugh? What would they never expect? What might they actually use?*

66.66% of the three kids leaned into it with gusto. The other 33.33% (yes that is the third one)? Not so much. Let's just say the not-so-subtle hints about the "joy of second-hand shopping" bounced off her like glass baubles on a tiled floor. She was less than impressed by it all. She unwrapped her gift with all the enthusiasm of someone opening a hefty tax bill and gave me a look that could have curdle brandy butter.

But the magic wasn't in the gifts it was in the storytelling, and in the fact that ten years later we're still laughing about her reaction.

Why this, why that? Why the ceramic frog? Because we all knew who was working through kissing a few frog trying to find Prince Charming.

The laughter that it all caused (for most of us) was worth more than any receipt.

Not every "budget treasure" was a hit. I once gave my daughter (yes, the 33.33% of my kids) a guitar from Cash Converters. In my head, it was thoughtful. In hers, it was child abuse. She unwrapped it, blinked twice, and looked at me like I'd just handed her a dead possum. I still think it was genius. She still insists it scarred her for life and has probably started drafting her very own memoir: *Christmases That Traumatised Me.*

That's the gamble with budget brilliance: sometimes you strike gold, and sometimes you accidentally gift-wrap a family trauma.

Either way, the stories last longer than the stuff. The disasters, in fact, make the best material. Because while shiny things fade and receipts get lost, the legend of *"Mum's Dead Possum Guitar"* will be retold at every family gathering *for generations still to come.* The Cash Converters guitar is still discussed at family gatherings never to be forgotten (or forgiven).

Quite frankly that make it one of the most memorable gifts I've ever given. It is the gift that keeps on giving, even though the guitar is long gone.

I call that Success!

The raw truth: I don't remember most of the shiny, expensive gifts I've ever given or received. I remember that jar of chocolate oranges. Why? Because they weren't trying to outshine the tree. They were created with love, and it was enough.

That tradition still lives on, passed to my kids, my cousins' kids, and even Auntie Peggy's grandkids. Chocolate Oranges are a huge part of our Christmases today. Christmas would not be the same without them.

Recently, I gifted the recipe to Debi, my cousin's wife and Aunty Peggy's daughter-in-law. Watching her face as she unwrapped it, realising she now held the key to a family treasure. It felt like handing over a piece of history. It wasn't just a recipe it was a connection to our roots. It came full circle.

Lesson: *The Power of Tinsel and Orange Peels*

The real power of Christmas isn't in the shine of the tinsel it's in the meaning we wrap beneath it. That resourcefulness, tradition, and the radical idea that a $10 handmade gift can outlast the thousand-dollar gadget that doesn't survive to New Year's. It's a love letter. A family recipe. An untold family story. There are the things that glitter can't disguise and the Tinsel Boa Constrictor can't squeeze the life out of.

Exercises to Complete

- **Chocolate Orange Legacy**
  Write about a handmade gift you once gave or received that mattered more than anything expensive. What made it unforgettable? What story did it carry? If it's part of a tradition—like those chocolate oranges—how could you keep it alive or pass it on?

- **The Budget Gift Rewind**
  Think back to a time you received a budget gift, handmade, second-hand, or so cheap it made you blush. How did you feel in that moment? Disappointed? Secretly delighted? Now fast-forward to today: would you feel differently if you got that same gift? What does that shift say about how you measure value?

Take 5 – Checklist

- **From Trash to Treasure**
  Go thrift shopping. Turn a thrift shop purchase into a gift, cookies in a jar, a spray-painted Salvos picture frame, a cutting from your garden

planted into a beautiful teacup, wrap up the most random book you can find. Put your heart, not your wallet, into it.

- **Tell the Origin Story**
  When you give a gift this year, especially a weird one—tell the story behind it.

- **Create a New (Imperfect) Tradition**
  Start a quirky, low-cost tradition. Matching thrift shop outfits? Reused wrapping paper? A communal box of regiftables? Make it yours and own the chaos.

- **Celebrate a Salvos Score**
  Gift or wear something secondhand with pride. If anyone raises an eyebrow, just call it a vintage heirloom.

- **Hide the Price Tags—Emotionally**
  Give something that costs nothing but heart: a playlist, a poem, a hand-written recipe card. (Bonus: no Klarna debt, no Boxing Day guilt.)

Quote of Choice

"The best gifts come from the heart, not the store." – **Sarah Dess**en

(And sometimes from the music section at Cash Converters—if you know where to look.)

CHAPTER FOUR

Shoes, Santa, and Second-Hand Barbies

Perspective really is everything. While some kids write letters to Santa demanding the latest gadgets or limited-edition sneakers, others like the children at Glen Lorne Orphanage in Zimbabwe wish for school shoes. Not flashy trainers, not toys that light up and sing, but plain, sturdy shoes to get them to school. Shoes that, when received, are met with toothy grins so wide they could light up the whole orphanage. Shoes that make each child stand a little taller and walk a little prouder knowing they have brand new shiny shoes for school.

Shoes are something most of us take for granted, but to genuinely appreciate them is a lesson in humility. My dad used to tell stories about walking to school barefoot through frost and snow in George a town infamous for being cold and wet. Even the car number plates seemed in on the misery; every vehicle began with *CAW*, which locals swore stood for "Cold and Wet." On their walks to school, his feet would get so numb he and his siblings would resort to, brace yourself, weeing on them just to keep warm. Can you imagine that?

The thought makes you shiver, but it's also a stark reminder of how something as simple as shoes can mean the world. Dad understood their value so deeply that he kept that pair of his Sunday school shoes from when he was about three. He would often show them to us a kids, tiny little relics preserved for decades, a reminder of his humble beginnings. That's appreciation for you. Pride woven into his shoes, the hardships they carried, and the gratitude they inspired, which lasted his lifetime.

Now, let's be honest: if some first-world kids unwrapped a pair of school shoes on Christmas morning, the huffing and eye-rolling would be so dramatic it would derail Santa's entire operation. The man in red would be out of a job faster than you can say *"reindeer rebellion."* You can almost hear the indignant cries: "Shoes? Seriously? Bruh! That's so unfair!" But...but... but... James got and electric scooter! This family sucks!

But for the kids at Glen Lorne, a new pair of shoes isn't a disappointment—it's a Christmas miracle. It means they've made it, that they get to go to school for another year. They will be walking tall and proud with every speck of dust polished off those new shoes. With those shoes those kids are gifted hope and opportunity for a better life.

I tried to instill the attitude of giving into my kids. Every December, I'd tell them that Santa's sleigh could only carry as much as they were willing to pass on to the orphanages. It became a ritual: little piles of toys on the floor, serious faces deciding which ones had earned a ticket into the new year. They were all under seven at the time, yet they approached it with a kind of cheerful practicality. A doll missing an arm? Off it went. A colouring book with only a few blank pages left? Perfect. To them, it wasn't about loss it was about making space for something new while giving someone else less fortunate a chance to enjoy what they'd outgrown. Some who was in real need.

At these orphanages or schools, those hand-me-downs were not seen as "used goods." It was treasure. A half-coloured book was an invitation to keep dreaming. A battered truck with chipped paint was still a vehicle for imagination. Watching my children proudly hand over bags of their old toys, I realised they were learning something a glossy department store ad couldn't teach, that generosity isn't about the size of the gift but the spirit in which it's given. Ask yourself this Christmas, if no one knew the gift was from you, would you still give the same gift? When we can give without needing the accolades that come from that giving then we know it is coming from the right place, and we are doing it with the right heart.

Fast forward again to our first, "First World Christmas". My kids came home announcing their school was collecting items for "the poor." Fantastic, I thought, what a perfect continuation of our tradition of passing on what we do not need. I pictured us lovingly packing up gently used toys for those who needed them more than us. But my elation popped like a cheap Christmas balloon when I read the note: *"New items only."*

Excuse me? New stuff? Tags still on? Bought specifically to give away? Suddenly, I could hear an imaginary mall Santa barking orders through mirrored aviators: *"Step away from the second-hand Barbie, lady. This sleigh is for fresh merchandise only."*

My brain short-circuited.

I turned to the kids and said, *"Well then, I guess we are the poor, move on, nothing more to give here."* My first set of knives and forks had come off the verge (street-side collection), along with half my furniture, lovingly hauled home during those tough first years of immigration. If "new" was the rule, then clearly, I'd been doing poverty all wrong.

It made me wonder: what exactly are we teaching our kids when we say that only "new" is good enough to give? Are we teaching generosity, or are we teaching appearances? Somewhere along the line, we started measuring kindness by its price tag rather than its impact. A $200 gadget wrapped in shiny foil looks impressive under the tree, but does it really mean more than the secondhand book your child clutched to their chest because you've written something personal inside the cover? We've blurred the line between giving with love and giving for show, between thoughtfulness and theatrics.

Who did that rule for "new items only" really serve? It's not the child in need who minds if their Barbie has a scuff on her knee, it's the giver who wants to feel like they've done something polished, something that looks good. It is charity wrapped up in the same glossy wrapping as everything else at Christmas, and in doing so, we've squeezed out the humanity in it. A child in real need does not need glossy wrapping.

Generosity was never meant to be curated. It was meant to be shared. True giving isn't about whether something is brand new, but whether it's useful, meaningful, and offered with love. Sometimes the most ordinary, imperfect gifts carry the greatest weight because they remind us we're seen, remembered, and worthy of someone else's care.

I've always loved receiving presents from my kids, not because of the present itself, but because of what they chose, and the thought tucked inside it. How do they perceive me? What was going through their little heads as they stood and decided, *this is Mum*. That, to me, was the real gift. They were gifts about value in the human sense. It was the glimpse into how my children saw me, how they loved me, and how they wanted to show up for me.

So, here's my advice: skip the Boxing Day sales.

Donate instead.

Look up Glen Lorne Orphanage in Harare, Zimbabwe or find a cause closer to your own heart. Save yourself the chaos of elbowing strangers for half-price air fryers and the regret of impulse-buys you didn't need in the first place. Instead of debating whether to splurge on a Bluetooth egg poacher or a voice-activated toilet brush, give to others who are hoping for the basics: a pair of shoes, a warm meal, or one small moment of joy.

Lesson: *Shoes, Santa, and Second-Hand Barbies*

Privilege doesn't always look like champagne flutes and private jets sometimes it's as ordinary as owning a pair of shoes, or having cutlery that didn't come off the side of the road. We get so caught up in what we think we lack be that money, status, matching linen, napkins etc that we forget how much we already have compared to others. This is a reminder to pause, shift our perspective, and recognise the quiet ways we're fortunate (especially when it comes to first-world privilege), even when life feels anything but luxurious. Gratitude is about noticing what's already good, and sharing it where we can.

Exercises to Complete

- **The Shoes That Changed It All**
  Write about a time you realised you'd been taking something small but

vital for granted (shoes, electricity, family, mental health, your ability to walk into a store and choose). What shifted in you? How could that awareness shape your choices this year?

- **Dear Santa, Skip Me This Year**
  Write a letter to "Santa" asking him to redirect one of your usual gifts (a bottle of perfume, a new gadget, another novelty mug) to someone who actually needs something. What would it look like to put your abundance to use? Then since Santa *isn't real, go do it yourself.*

- **The "New Only" Policy**
  Reflect on the moment someone rejected the idea of second-hand gifts. What does that reveal about how we define "giving"? Now, rewrite the rules in your own words what message would you want them to hear instead? Then, make it real: create a list of three charities, causes, or individuals you'd like to support this year. Don't stop at money; think time, kindness, or practical help.

Take 5 – Checklist

- **Choose One Gift to Give Away**
  Find something you were planning to keep or regift within your circle and donate it instead. Even if it's small. Even if it stings a little. Especially then.

- **Teach Giving, Not Guilt**
  Invite your kids, friends, or family to join you in a giving tradition cleaning out toys, making care packages, or writing letters to someone forgotten.

- **Pause Before You Swipe**
  Next time you're tempted to buy something unnecessary "because it's Christmas," pause. Ask: *Do I really need this? Or do I just need to feel*

better? Then redirect that energy into something more meaningful.

- **Name the Real Gift**

  Write down one thing you have that money can't buy. Health, chosen family, freedom, laughter. Stick it on the fridge. That's your true wish list. (If you're really invested, read *You Are Really Rich: You Just Don't Know It Yet* by Steve Henry, a book my kids have heard me quote approximately one million times.)

- **Reach Out to the Forgotten**

  Text or call someone who might not be in the holiday "inner circle." A widowed neighbour. An old friend. A "Courtenay" (More on that to come). Be the bridge.

Quote of Choice

"No one has ever become poor by giving." – **Anne Frank**

(Because the opposite is true, the more you give, the richer you become.)

CHAPTER FIVE

The Price of Joy and Crippling Financial Anxiety

A h, Christmas the season of joy, togetherness, and crippling financial anxiety. It's funny, isn't it? The lengths we go to ensure the kids have *enough* presents under the tree, as if their love for us depends on the quantity, and the quality, of what we've wrapped. By "funny," I mean the kind of funny where you laugh hysterically, clutching your receipt, wondering how on earth you just spent $150 on stocking fillers.

Stocking fillers! Those little bits and bobs that are meant to be cheap, cheerful, and utterly forgettable. Yet somehow, they've collectively conspired to ruin your Christmas budget time and time again. Suddenly, you're standing there, breaking into a sweat, a full-blown hot flash creeping up your spine, and you're thinking, *Is this menopause or just the financial panic setting in?*

You tell yourself it's fine. Just a little warm in here. Maybe the store's heating is on just too high, or the air conditioner is not on enough! But then your ears start glowing like Rudolph's nose on overdrive, sweat beads appear on your upper lip, and your chest feels like it's hosting a small but determined campfire.

You start mentally retracing your steps. Okay, there were the novelty socks. The chocolate Santas. The miniature Lego set that wasn't really "miniature" in price. The scented candles because... why not? Then you remember the pack of bath bombs shaped like reindeer heads. What child even uses bath bombs?! But it's too late now. They're in the bag, along with a weird plastic slinky you were convinced would be a hit. You're sweating harder now, fanning yourself with the receipt and whispering, *It's fine, it's Christmas. Everyone overspends. Fuck me,* you realise in panic there's no difference between hormonal chaos and the realization that you've spent the grocery budget on stocking fillers shaped like miniature reindeer butts.

It's not fine.

You've been duped by the illusion of "festive cheer." You know it, the cashier knows it, and the bath bombs know it. Yet, the madness doesn't stop there. You've convinced yourself you need just a little more. What's a Christmas stocking if it's not overflowing like Santa's sleigh on all those pretty little Christmas cards? So you hit another shop, adding glitter pens, novelty erasers, and a light-up keychain that will break before it ever finds a key.

By the time you're done, your trolley's heaving with "essential" – not! stocking fillers, and your sense of regret is bursting out of you like cheap prosecco – fizzy, dramatic, and impossible to contain. At least the reindeer-shaped bath bombs will look festive as they dissolve into the tub, kind of like my will to live after seeing that total.

You try to justify it by telling yourself it's Christmas, it's for the kids, it's tradition, but deep down you know it's none of that. It's capitalism dressed in tinsel, that sly little pickpocket with one hand offering joy and the other quietly emptying your wallet whistling all the way to the checkout.

After evaluating all this madness one year, I made an important decision. F* you, Santa, I thought. You're not getting all the credit for my blood, sweat, and financial panic attacks.

From that year forth, Santa was relegated to the "shite gifts", you know, the practical stuff no one really wants but everyone needs – new socks, a toothbrush, deodorant, and for good measure. Sometimes I would even throw in all items the listed on that year's school stationery list, along with extra maths lessons for good measure. Nothing captures the magic of the season like algebra wrapped in glossy paper. Joy to the world, here comes trigonometry!

The fun gifts, the ones that made my kids' faces light up like the Christmas tree, those came from me. With my name, front and centre, written in ink so bold it could be seen from space. I wasn't about to spend my hard-earned cash and let some imaginary fat man dressed in red take the credit. Oh no, not this year. Not this mother.

Santa, bless his overworked soul, was no longer the bringer of joy, he could keep his cheap thrills and cavity prevention campaigns. By the time I was done rebranding the jolly old man, his gift list read less like a Christmas miracle and more like the school stationery order form. I swear, half his sack looked like a Kmart back-to-school special. Honestly? It was genius. The kids still got their stockings filled, but the thrill of toothpaste and long division was safely pinned on the big guy in red, leaving me free to swoop in later with the fun stuff.

That was it from now on, the new Christmas hierarchy I made sure the kids knew exactly where the sparkle came from and just in case there was ever any doubt, I would throw in something truly uncool, a gift so aggressively practical it could crush any lingering belief in Santa's sparkle. That sealed the deal. Santa did the boring stuff; I did the fun. Santa never stood a chance.

And you know what? It worked. The kids figured it out pretty quickly: who was cooler, me or the big guy in red? (Hint: it wasn't the one handing out deodorant and math workbooks.) Or at least, that's what I told myself while laughing at their faces as they unwrapped the toothpaste. No more of that old story where he gets the credit and I get the credit-card debt. Ho Ho Ho, Santa, who's laughing now? It's me, sitting here with a glass of wine and the satisfaction of knowing I finally beat the system. You get the cookies; I get the glory. Fair trade, I'd say.

One year, in my desperate quest to meet the mythical standard of "enough," I did something truly absurd: I sold our wedding rings. Mine and his. Yes, he-who-shall-not-be-named made his unwitting contribution to Christmas that year, finally useful for something. I can still picture myself at the gold trader's counter, sliding those rings across the glass and chanting in my head, *This is for the kids. It's for Christmas. It's fine.* Fine? It was *insane.* I'd essentially traded "forever" (though, let's be honest, that ship had already hit the iceberg and was halfway to the ocean floor) for "unwrap faster." A lifetime promise pawned for five minutes of paper-tearing euphoria.

At the time, it felt noble. Heroic, even. Like I was some festive warrior-queen, sacrificing her crown jewels trading sentiment for survival to keep the household running and the myth of holiday happiness intact. I walked out clutching that small wad of cash proof that I could still pull off a miracle, even if it came at the cost of my sanity and a few grams of gold.

The best part? I didn't even buy anything extraordinary. No ponies or diamond-studded roller skates. Just toys plastic things that beeped, buzzed, and broke before New Year's. Yet, I felt victorious walking away with the cash in hand, ready to prove to the kids, the world, and Santa himself that I had been a very good mum. Which, when you think about it, is completely absurd. *Prove it? To whom?* To a fictional man in a red suit who's been taking credit for my hard work since the dawn of their childhood? To the mums at school whose trees look like they were decorated by stylists instead of toddlers on a sugar high? To society, the great, faceless judgemental crowd.

The whole thing was ridiculous, but there I was, desperate for a gold star. I wanted someone, anyone, to see the effort. The sleepless nights, the budget acrobatics, the emotional gymnastics of pretending I wasn't drowning in both debt and tinsel. I wanted validation, not presents. I wanted a standing ovation from the North Pole. It's funny, in a bleak sort of way how easily we fall into that trap of trying to *prove* our love, our worth, our "good mum" status with ... plastic.

Let me tell you, I'm not alone in this madness. A friend once told me her own tale of financial desperation, and it was so ridiculous, I nearly choked on my tea. She'd maxed out her credit card on Christmas shopping and decided to sell her car. Not to downgrade, mind you, but to fund the perfect Christmas. Picture this: she's wrapping gifts in her lounge, smugly satisfied with her generosity, while her husband peers out the window wondering why their driveway is suddenly so empty. *"Oh, the car? Yeah, I sold it. But look at this 8-foot inflatable Santa for the front yard!"* Apparently, a towering air-filled Saint Nick was essential to the festive experience.

We laughed about it later how she spent the next six months trying to fix her misjudgement, all for the sake of a Christmas that was gone in a flash. But isn't that the point? The stress, the debt, the absurdity, it's all for a single day that no one remembers as clearly as the chaos it caused.

So, why do we do it? Why do we put ourselves under this pressure to buy more, spend more, and give more than we can afford? Is it because we think our love needs to be wrapped up and labelled "from Santa"? Or because we're competing in some invisible contest to prove we're "good enough"?

If we're honest, we're not just doing it for the kids. We're doing it for ourselves, to silence that inner voice that whispers, *Are you enough?*

We are enough, just by showing up, even if we are empty handed.

Whether we wrap three gifts or thirty, whether we spend hundreds, make an IOU book, or—God help us—sell our jewellery (or cars, apparently), it doesn't change a thing. The best gifts were never under the tree. They were never something you could scan at the checkout or wrap in sparkly paper. They're in the small, ridiculous, unforgettable moments we spend together. They're in the stories we retell every year, the ones that get more dramatic and less accurate with time.

Sometimes we discover our children have been paying much closer attention than we ever intended. My daughter once did exactly that. She made an IOU card for her boyfriend—sweet, handmade, full of glitter and adolescent sincerity. "IOU one hug, redeemable anytime." Cute, right? Then came "IOU one back rub," "IOU one home-cooked dinner," and—oh yes—"IOU one surprise."

Needless to say, the boy was thrilled. I was horrified.

There was a lot of watchful parenting that Christmas—me, hovering in the background like a paranoid elf, nervously eyeing every interaction, waiting to see which IOU might be cashed in next. "One hug"? Fine. "One back rub"? Questionable. "One surprise"? Absolutely not under my roof.

Those moments—the chaos, the connection, the shared exhaustion, *that's* the real magic. It's the kind of gift you can't return, can't re-gift, and definitely can't buy in bulk. Everything else fades, breaks, or ends up in landfill. Those memories? They're the only things that actually last.

So, this Christmas, let's laugh at the absurdity. Let's question the madness. Let's stop sacrificing our sanity, and our jewellery, for one day of orchestrated joy. Please, for heaven's sake, let's keep the rings, even if they did buy that amazing dinosaur. Okay, maybe that dinosaur was worth it. The way Kiffy's face lit up, pure delight, pure magic, that moment was everything. He believed the world was wonderful and that I (and by I, I mean not Santa – he gives boring gifts) was an absolute legend. I'll never regret that. Though yes, that poor creature now lies somewhere in a landfill, buried alongside the ghosts of Christmas past.

But next time? I'll find a way to make that magic without needing to pawn the past. I'll skip the gold trader's counter and keep both my rings and my sense of reason.

Lesson: *The Price of Joy and Crippling Financial Anxiety*

There's no sticker price for love, but damn if we don't keep trying to swipe it anyway. This chapter is a brutally funny look at the financial insanity we justify in the name of "Christmas magic" maxed-out cards, panic buying, emotional bribery via bath bombs, and yes, even pawning wedding rings. It's about the impossible standard of "enough" and the lie that joy has to come with a price tag. The only thing you're buying is anxiety and novelty socks no one asked for.

Exercises to Complete

- **Receipts of Regret**
  List the top five things you've bought in a Christmas panic (yes, include the reindeer bath bombs). Next to each, write down what you were actually trying to feel/ or create. Then ask: was it worth it? (Answer: probably not but at least it smelled like cinnamon.)

- **Dear Santa, You're Fired**
  Write a declaration officially stripping Santa of all credit for your emotional labour and financial sacrifice. From now on, socks and school books = North Pole. Joy and surprises = your name in bold. Reclaim your narrative.

- **The Cost of "Enough"**
  What did chasing "enough" actually cost you -financially, emotionally, mentally? Write yourself a mini invoice. Then rip it up and write a refund policy for your sanity.

- **If Love Had a Budget**
  Imagine you only had $10 to spend on each person. What would you give to make them feel loved? Now actually do one yes, even if it's just a handmade IOU card covered in glitter glue and chaos.

Take 5 – Checklist

- **Hide the Credit Card**
  For 24 hours, resist the impulse to "just grab one more thing." You're not fixing anyone's childhood with a scented candle.

- **Flip the Gift Script**
  Give something that costs $0 but holds real meaning a letter, a photo (PG Rated), a recipe, a playlist. Emotional ROI: through the roof.

- **Celebrate Your Inner Scrooge**
  Pick one thing you will *not* buy this year—and feel smugly proud about it. Bonus points if it's usually a guilt gift.

- **Budget, But Make It Emotional**
  Set a feelings budget. How much peace, fun, and rest do you want? Build your holiday around that instead of sales.

- **Wear the Damn Socks**
  Whatever weird, practical gift you got (or gave), rock it proudly. Socks are underrated. So are you.

Quote of Choice

"Too many people spend money they haven't earned, to buy things they don't want, to impress people they don't like." – **Will Rogers**

(Which sums up the entire Boxing Day sales in one sentence.)

CHAPTER SIX

Under the Mistletoe with My Shadow

N ow, let's move on, shall we? What a "shite" time of the year. Honestly, I'm not surprised my heart got drop-kicked across the festive finish line at Christmas. Yip flying through the air and landing squarely in the smouldering ruins of my meticulously planned holiday. I didn't just get dumped, I got dumped right before Christmas. It wasn't just a breakup, it was a festive KO (Knock Out) the kind you don't come back from with a bit of tinsel and a glass of mulled wine. One minute you're basting the ham and feeling smug about your trifle layers; the next, you're staring at an emotional crime scene, wondering if the cranberry sauce is worth finishing.

It felt like the whole season had been tackled to the ground, stockings and all. For a split second I honestly wondered if I should cancel the holiday altogether set fire to the tree and wrap myself in the Christmas lights to see if I could short-circuit the whole neighbourhood.

It was like the universe doubled down and thought, "*You know what would make this season extra special? A side of heartbreak with that turkey.*"

Let me set the scene. My mum was out from Zimbabwe, bringing her brand of maternal wisdom and passive-aggressive holiday commentary. Paul's kids had flown in from various corners of the world, some with extra partners in tow. My kids were here too. The house was full. That made three adults and eight adult children, ranging from their early 20s to hormonal teens all crammed into one small three bedroom house. It was a seething pit of Christmas anxiety waiting to erupt.

Erupt it did.

There's a special kind of cruelty in Christmas breakups, the tinsel still twinkles, the fairy lights mock you with their relentless cheer and everywhere you look, people are coupling up under mistletoe. I was standing in that kitchen, holding a spatula with the emotional stability of a snowflake in a heatwave wondering how to keep going. I had just been left alone with pursed lips under the mistletoe, my only company my shadow.

It was the kind of dramatic, well-timed exit that belongs in a bad rom-com except I didn't get the reconciliation scene at the end. No last-minute dash to the airport, no heartfelt speech in the rain, no sweeping gesture to win me back. Just me, standing in the middle of a house full of half-decorated chaos, feeling like someone had yanked the rug out from under my life and replaced it with shards of tinsel, disappointment, and that damn Boa Constrictor.

It had slithered in without warning, coiling itself around my chest and squeezing tighter with every forced smile and every fake "Merry Christmas" I had to mutter. So what did I do? I just kept cooking, because what else can you do? When your world collapses mid-roast, you cling to the illusion of control. You baste, you stir, you glaze like a crazy. You keep busy so you don't have to think. Because if you stop for too long, you might start screaming, or worse.

By mid-afternoon, I was Googling, *"Is it too late to become a nun?"* while also considering whether locking myself in the bedroom with a bottle of gin and several movies could count as a "new Christmas tradition."

I think I fell in love with Paul-my "Crazy 'Orse," the moment we met, and for a while it felt like the universe was finally on my side. He matched my spirit, my energy, my wit-a rare trifecta. But there was always that one thing, wild and untameable, that kept me slightly off balance. A restless streak that thrilled me and unsettled me all at once, leaving me in a constant state of unease, like waiting for a storm you know will eventually break.

While he made me uneasy, he also made me question everything. He made me believe that maybe chaos could be comfort, that maybe love wasn't meant to feel safe, but alive. That was intoxicating until it wasn't. Because loving someone like Paul was like standing barefoot in a lightning storm: electrifying, unforgettable, and bound to leave a mark.

But he also made me rethink what life could be, peeling away the nonsense and showing me what was real. Paul was the one who saw through the tinsel and ribbons, who reminded me that Christmas-or life-wasn't about the glitter, but about grounding.

He had this way of stripping back the chaos, peeling away the noise and distractions, until only the essentials were left.

With him, it wasn't about the showy centrepiece on the table or whether the presents matched the catalogue spreads it was about the laughter echoing around the room, the quiet moments when the world slowed down, the feeling of belonging.

It wasn't just about Christmas; it was about everything. He pushed me to question what really mattered, to see through the smoke and mirrors of perfection, and to find value in the messy, unpolished, real stuff. It was about people. People were important.

Ironic, really, that he managed to ruin Christmas the one time I actually felt at home.

It was as if he'd orchestrated the ultimate lesson without even meaning to: just when you think you've found home in someone else, life finds a way to remind you that home has to come from within you.

Okay, that lesson didn't drift in gently. It thundered in like a Christmas cyclone, complete with lightning and chaos, impossible to ignore. It tore through everything I thought was secure, scattering love, plans, and perfectly folded napkins alike. But ultimately emotional storms don't just wreck, they reveal. When the noise had died down, we finally see with startling clarity what's worth rebuilding and what we should've let blow away a long ago.

Trying to hold my heart together while keeping Christmas from collapsing? Hard. Trying to do that *and* make it perfect? Bloody impossible. Me? I floated through it all like a Christmas ghost, smiling just enough to stop anyone asking questions. My insides felt like a snow globe someone had shaken too hard, but I couldn't let the cracks show. Not on Christmas. Of bloody course not. I felt ridiculous. Who gets dumped at Christmas? It felt like such a cliché. One day before Christmas, and a houseful of people, all blissfully oblivious to the fact that my world had just imploded.

Every time the wave of emotions threatened to crash over me, I'd breathe, sip some wine, and remind myself: *Focus.* You can lose it later. Right now, there's trifle to serve and wrapping paper multiplying like rabbits across the floor. So I smiled, stirred, and played hostess, pretending the sugar and the sarcasm would somehow hold me together. That's what women do at Christmas, we perform triage with tinsel, patch the cracks with pavlova, and call it holiday spirit.

That Christmas, diazepam became my best friend. Not a casual acquaintance, a best friend. The kind who doesn't ask questions, just quietly does the job. I'd pop a tablet, take a sip of wine, and think, *Right, time to be festive!* Festive, in this case, meant not losing my temper when the chorus of *"Mum, Mum, Mum—Dad's is better!"* started up for the fourth time that day. Better food, better tree, better presents apparently at Dad's, everything was better. *"Oh really?"* I wanted to snap. *"Well, maybe at Dad's, Santa doesn't forget to bring deodorant and math workbooks."* Instead, I smiled through gritted teeth, muttered, *"That's nice, darling,"* and mentally cursed he-who-shall-not-be-named for living rent-free in my kids' holiday memories as some kind of festive superhero.

Let me tell you: diazepam gives you a kind of zen you don't know you need until you're staring at a burnt tray of vegetables while kids argue over whose fart is loudest. It's the only reason I didn't launch the tray across the kitchen when someone chirped, *"Isn't it time to be jolly?"*

It's also why I managed to calmly clear wrapping paper carnage without locking myself in the pantry with a bottle of whiskey. Instead, I plastered on a smile and told the kids how proud I was of their fart-volume competition. Parenting at its finest.

The best part? When my mum spotted the pill bottle on the counter. She squinted at the label, raised an eyebrow, and said, *"What's this, Karie? Christmas spirit in pill form?"* I nodded solemnly. *"Mum, it's the only reason I haven't thrown the turkey out the window."* She nodded, empathetic as ever.

By the end of the day, the kids were happy and miraculously the house and tree were still standing. I, however, was running purely on adrenaline, and the faint hum of survival instinct. Emotionally wrecked but somehow still upright, I crawled into bed, whispered a shaky little prayer to the gods of endurance, and muttered, "Thank you, diazepam. You're the real MVP."

Now, before anyone gets the wrong idea, let me be clear: I'm not advocating for pharmaceuticals or Pinot Grigio as a sustainable coping strategy. I'm just saying that, in the battle of Christmas versus my mental stability, a mild sedative and a glass of something cold formed a temporary peace treaty.

As I lay there that night, the absurdity wasn't lost on me. My world had just shattered, and yet there I was, fussing over table settings and making sure the candles were lit at just the right angle, as if symmetry could somehow save me. Looking back, it's almost laughable how I thought perfection might hold me together while my heart was in pieces. We cling to "perfect" like it's a life raft, when really, it's all about the people who stay. I realised something beautiful in its simplicity: survival itself was enough.

Rock bottom clears the view. My mum was still there steady, irreplaceable. I still had myself. I later learned that time *with myself* was the best gift I could ever give. It didn't come wrapped in a bow, it didn't come with a receipt, and it sure as hell wasn't Instagram-worthy but it was real.

More than anything, that time made me question. Not just him – but everything. Was it me? Was it Christmas? Was it life's twisted way of reminding me that happiness is fleeting? Or was it simply bad timing, cruelly wrapped in a shiny bow? Whatever it was, I found myself standing in the wreckage, realising that in the long run, losing Paul gave me back something I didn't even know I'd lost—myself.

Sure, I spent that Christmas holding back tears, pretending to care about everyone's fourth helping of trifle, and knocking back diazepam like it was an old friend. But looking back, I can see it wasn't the end of the world, it was the beginning of a new one. A world where I no longer needed someone else to define my happiness.

And you know what? It didn't break me. It cracked me, yes – but through those cracks, something real began to grow. That Christmas, for all its pain, gave me a gift I didn't recognise at the time: the permission to stop carrying everything. To let the façade fall away and sit with what was real, even when it hurt. To finally stop giving my heart to people who didn't know how to hold it.

So don't let the empty space beside you convince you that you are less, or that your worth depends on someone else's presence. The real gift isn't who's standing next to you, it's who you become when no one is there at all.

There's a quiet power in learning to stand on your own, even in the loneliest moments. It's not easy, God knows, it's not but that's where the magic happens. In the silences that first feel deafening, you start to hear your own voice. The one drowned out for years by noise, expectation, and the need to keep it all together.

When you stop waiting for someone else to make you whole, you realise you were never incomplete. You learn to fill your own cup, to take yourself to dinner, to dance in the kitchen like no one's watching because no one is, and that's the beauty. You discover that being alone isn't failure, it's freedom. Freedom to love yourself in the way you've always deserved, without compromise, without apology.

So, if you find yourself standing under the mistletoe this Christmas with no one to kiss, remember this: you are enough. More than enough. You are the love you've been searching for, the partner you've been waiting for, and the person who will never leave you standing there alone.

Light the candles. Pour yourself a glass of something you love. Raise a toast to the most important relationship you'll ever have: the one with yourself. Because when you truly love who you are, every moment Christmas included becomes a celebration of the home you've built within.

Lesson Learned: Under the Mistletoe with My Shadow

Sometimes the most important person you'll ever spend Christmas with... is yourself. And no, not in a bubble-bath-with-a-face-mask, self-care-is-sexy Instagram post kind of way, but in the raw, messy, *"what the actual hell just happened?"* kind of way. This chapter is about abandonment, heartbreak, keeping it together for the sake of the trifle, and ultimately discovering that the only arms you need to fall into are your own. When the mistletoe is empty, the pavlova has collapsed, and your heart feels like it got trampled by a rogue reindeer – what's left is you. And that's enough.

Exercises to Complete

- **The Scene of the (Emotional) Crime**
  Recount a time when someone walked out, let you down, or left you

holding the tinsel alone. Where were you? What were you clutching (literally or metaphorically)? Then write how you showed up for yourself anyway even if it was just surviving the day.

- **Your "Rock Bottom" Starter Pack**
  List five things that kept you going in a moment you felt your lowest. A person, a playlist, a pet, a sarcastic inner monologue. These are your emergency glitter grenades. Name them. Honour them.

- **The Mirror Isn't the Villain**
  Write a letter to the version of yourself who stood in that kitchen, spoon in one hand and shattered heart (or hopes) in the other. Tell her what you know now: that she is still whole, even when she feels broken. That she doesn't need someone else to validate her, fix her, or carry her. Remind her that the mirror is not an enemy, it's a reflection of a woman strong enough to survive this moment and love herself through it. Say it with love. Say it with sass. Say it so she never forgets: *you can trust yourself, you can choose yourself, and you will always be enough.*

Take 5 – Checklist

- **Toast to Yourself First**
  On Christmas—or hell, any day—pour the first glass of wine, juice, or ginger tea for you. Don't wait. Don't ask. Cheers to your own resilience.

- **Reclaim the Space**
  Stand in a spot that once broke your heart (the kitchen, the tree, the mistletoe) and declare it yours again. Out loud. Bonus points for theatrics.

- **Schedule the Ugly Cry**
  You're allowed to feel it. Block out an hour to sob into a pillow, curse the season, and eat pavlova straight from the bowl. Call it healing.

- **Find Your "Paul-Proof" Joy**
  Do one thing that makes you feel grounded, something no partner, no ex, no holiday expectation can take away from you.

- **Write a "Thanks for Leaving" Note**
  Write (and maybe burn) a sarcastically grateful note to the person who left or let you down. *"Thanks for the life lesson, the eye bags, and the emotional growth. Sincerely, the upgraded version of me."*

Quote of Choice

"You alone are enough. You have nothing to prove to anybody." – Maya Angelou

(And certainly not to someone who left the day before Christmas. Because it turns out, I was always the gift.)

CHAPTER SEVEN

"No Cash, No Presents, Just the Truth"

W hat is it with the lack of appreciation? It's the gift that keeps on giving, isn't it? The sting doesn't just hurt, it lodges itself in your heart like a splinter: tiny, sharp, and impossible to ignore. It keeps on niggling, the way a stone in your shoe ruins an otherwise lovely walk. You can still keep moving, smile at people you pass, even convince yourself it's fine but every step, every shift, there it is again, digging in, reminding you it's still there.

That's what lack of appreciation feels like. It's not a dramatic stab wound you can point to and say, "Look! I'm bleeding!" It's the quiet, persistent irritation that never fully heals because no one else even notices it exists. You make the effort, pour your heart into it, and instead of being met with gratitude, you get silence or worse, indifference. And silence, my friends, echoes louder than any thankless mutter.

Christmas, as I keep batting on about, is supposed to be about time together love, laughter, and the kind of memories you can't buy. Fleeting, imperfect moments that stay with you long after the gifts are forgotten or the tree is out on the curb.

It's bonding. That's the point, isn't it? Christmas makes up for all the other times of year when we're scattered, distracted, and swallowed whole by the chaos of everyday life. It's the pause button, the moment we all sit still long enough to actually look around the room and think, Ah! yes, these are my people. This is my Tribe. The ones who know my secrets, my quirks, my laugh, my temper. The ones who would bail me out of jail or, help hide the bodies if it came to that.

The reminder that you belong to a little tribe of misfits who'll show up when it counts. Christmas, at least in its best form, is supposed to be about that: time together, love, laughter, and the kind of memories you can't buy. Fleeting, imperfect, ridiculous moments that outlast every candle, every cracker, every over-glazed ham.

For me, those moments aren't just important-they're everything. They're the anchor points in a world that so often feels untethered. Proof that even when life scatters us in a thousand directions, there's still a table we return to-a place where laughter stitches us back together and we remember who we are, and who we are to each other. This is our tribe. Our beautiful, imperfect, slightly chaotic tribe, that accepts you for who you are and that's what makes it home.

I pour my heart into Christmas. Every detail, every dish, every daft little tradition, it's all stitched together with love and a slightly manic determination. I want Christmas to be the kind of day my kids and family look back on and smile. The sort of memory that still glows decades later, even when both the tree and I have both gone a bit crooked. I want them to remember the smell of the roast in the oven, the crack of laughter after a truly awful cracker joke, the ridiculous games. I want them to remember the warmth, the noise, most of all the sense of belonging. The sense that, just for that one day, everything and everyone was exactly where they were meant to be.

Why? Because that's what I remember from my own childhood. Not the gifts, I can't recall a single one, but the moments. Those little golden threads woven into a tapestry of belonging.

The sound of someone laughing so hard they couldn't breathe.

Chairs scraping against the floor as we finally sat down and the clinking of glasses joining in like a chorus.

The faint hum of a familiar song on the radio, the smell of roast potatoes mingling with the laughter of people who knew how to love loudly and imperfectly.

The house would be alive with the kind of chaos that only families can create. It is so hard to put your finger on it exactly but essentially it is in the glow of togetherness, just being together and all the chaos that is created by that.

The unpolished, unscripted moments that root themselves deep in memory and grow into something bigger than the day itself. Those are the moments that stay and weave their threads of laughter, warmth, and connection into the tapestry to keeping it from unravelling.

In those moments, he was always there, my dad raising his glass like he was addressing the United Nations. He wasn't just toasting; he was delivering a speech, complete with a booming voice and a twinkle in his eye, as if the fate of the world hinged on his words. "To family!" he'd declare with the gravitas of a man announcing world peace, pausing just long enough for us to roll our eyes and stifle our giggles. Every year, without fail, he played his part as the self-appointed Chief Toastmaster of Christmas, had lopsided on this head and his cheeks slightly pink, determined to turn a simple moment into an occasion worthy of history books.

My mum? She'd roll her eyes at his theatrics while secretly loving every second. Dad, the grand orator, and Mum, the secretly pleased muse pretending not to enjoy the spotlight as he toasted her culinary skills. It was the rhythm of belonging to a tribe, to something bigger than just you. It was the ritual of love, disguised as speeches and eye-rolls, laughter, debate and clinking glasses.

Those memories? Untouchable. Etched so deeply into me that not even dementia can scrub them away. If one day my mind loses the details, I know I'll still feel the warmth of those moments in the corners of my soul.

And that's the reason I put so much effort into Christmas. Not for Instagram applause or some Pinterest-perfect table, but for the threads. The tiny, unpolished bits that stitch us together as a family. The laughter that erupts when someone trips over the dog. The silence that feels like peace, not awkwardness. The kids giggling so hard they forget the fight they had five minutes earlier.

You can't manufacture those moments. You can't plan them or schedule them. They only bloom when you're actually present. Not "present" as in scrolling through Instagram to compare yourself to everyone else's highlight reel, but present as in breathing, noticing, soaking up what's in front of you.

So, when people skip dinner, miss the toast, or don't even bother to call, it's not just a missed event it's a hole in the tapestry. A gap where something beautiful should have been. You can almost see it: a frayed thread in the tapestry dangling, an empty space where colour and laughter should have been woven in. A gap that doesn't stay neatly contained. It tugs at the whole fabric, weakening it, making the rest of the pattern wobble just a little.

Because it's never just one dinner, is it? It's the echo of all the other moments that could have been. It's looking around the room and feeling not just who is there, but who isn't and realising that their *chosen* absence changes everything.

Those gaps don't close on their own. You can't patch them later with a quick text or a belated, "Sorry I couldn't make it." The moment has passed. The memory that could have been stitched into the tapestry is gone, leaving only that hole, that ache, that sting of being the one who showed up while someone else couldn't be bothered.

That's why it hurts when people don't see it the same way. When they skip the dinner, miss the toast, or forget to call.

Those little moments aren't just about Christmas they're about life they're the threads that strengthen the fabric of who we are together. That's the only thing we'll have left when all the presents are unwrapped and the chairs around the table aren't as full as they used to be.

That's where the true ache sets in, the difference between those who choose not to be there and those who simply can't. The first is absence wrapped in indifference. It's a conscious decision, a shrug of convenience. They miss the dinner because they chose not to carry the small weight of effort it takes to stay connected.

It's not life pulling them away, it's indifference. It's the quiet cruelty of someone who doesn't care enough to want that connection, who doesn't understand that showing up isn't about the food or the table, it's about choosing to be part of something bigger than themselves, being there for the other people sitting round the table.

You can't help but feel the sting. Because when you've poured yourself into creating moments of belonging, and someone treats them like an optional extra, it's not just disappointment, it's grief. Not for what's missing on the table, but for what's missing in the space between people.

Then there are the others, the ones who'd give anything to be there but cannot. The ones who *never chose* their absence. Their empty chair isn't a decision, it's a wound. You can still see their plate, still hear their laugh echoing faintly in the spaces between conversation, as if the air itself remembers them. Those are the deep gaps, the ones that stretch through the years and tug at your heart every time you pass their photo or use the old serving spoon they once insisted was "the good one."

That's the cruel beauty of time, isn't it? It teaches you to tell the difference between someone who's missing by circumstance and someone who's missing by choice. One leaves you aching with love; the other, with disappointment. One you grieve; the other, you have to learn to let go of.

So that's why every shared moment matters. Every toast, every clinking glass, every silly game, every burst of laughter, it all counts. Why? Because once it's gone, you can't stitch it back in.

So why am I here, running the entire pantomime solo, lead actor, director, stagehand, and audience all rolled into one? Because of that tapestry. It's not about keeping up appearances; it's about keeping the threads intact, weaving the pattern. Someone has to hold the needle. So I do. Even when it's exhausting. Even when it feels like no one notices.

One day the kids will see that this tapestry of effort and love isn't woven from tradition or duty, but from devotion to them. When the time comes, I hope they'll pick up the needle or the thread, whatever you want to call it and start weaving their own version. It may look different, looser around the edges, maybe even brighter in places, but that's the point. It will be theirs.

We will be there in those quiet moments when we catch ourselves smiling across the room, the kind of smile that says, *Look at us.* All these beautiful, imperfect humans somehow coming together to create this messy, magical thing we call family. That's why I keep the show running. That's why I keep frantically stitching.

Since immigrating, I've been alone in a way I never was back home. No uncles booming with laughter, no aunts gossiping in the kitchen. Just me, needle in hand, trying to stitch together two worlds: the family I left behind and the one I'm building here. So when people don't show up not physically, not emotionally it feels like a double rejection.

But I keep sewing anyway. Because love, connection, belonging—they're all handmade. Maybe that's the legacy I'm really leaving behind: proof that even when it feels lonely, you can still make something whole out of what's left.

Take my kids and their partners. I adore them. Worship the ground they walk on. Once upon a time, I was their whole universe. Now? I'm "optional viewing," the side character in the movie of their lives. Sure, I'm supposed to embrace that whole *Let Them* philosophy. Let Them not Visit, Let Them not Call, Let Them not even send a Pigeon. But Let Me Tell You what's not happening: unopened gifts sitting under my tree like abandoned puppies. Not this year, not this mum. Those holes are not making their way into my tapestry.

No sir! There's a new tradition being woven into our tapestry, one that applies to everyone in my orbit, not just the kids. Friends, family, neighbours, that one who only appears when there's food involved, listen closely. If anyone dares to ghost me this Christmas, they don't get the goodies. I redistribute those gifts faster than you can say "holiday spirit." No swooping in for your annual appearance like Santa with commitment issues. If you can't be bothered to call, connect, or contribute, then congratulations, you've officially been removed from the Nice List. Presents go to people who actually show up or, frankly, to me because yes, I deserve them. You snooze, you lose. It's called "consequences", and that's my new favourite holiday tradition.

In actual fact, to anyone expecting to treat this Christmas like a McDonald's pick-up window (you know who you are!) swing by, grab the gifts, toss a quick "Merry Christmas," and speed off, you are in for a surprise. The drive through window is going to be closed. This is supposed to be Christmas, not a drive-through service. There'll be no gifts or cash handed over with a smile while you're already halfway out the door, and certainly nothing delivered via Uber Christmas. This year, I'm not chasing. I'm not calling. I'm not begging for scraps of anyone's time. Nope. The next time anyone who dares, hear from me will be when they each unwrap this book on Christmas morning. That's right, no Salvos treasures, no last-minute panic gifts from the "seasonal" aisle, just *Oh F*ck It's Christmas* starring them. And no as I said, I'm not changing names. If you made the cut, congratulations. If not... well, maybe read between the lines.

Think of it as a wake-up call. A stocking stuffer for the soul delivered with a Ho Ho Ho. Suddenly, even a $2 Salvos mug is starting to look like treasure compared to the truth wrapped in glitter and sarcasm.

So, here's my festive message: ***show up.***

Not for the gifts.

Not for the food.

Show up for the people who love you, for the ones who keep the traditions alive, for the tribe that makes you more than just a lone thread. Because one day you'll look around that table and realise someone's chair is empty and no amount of belated "Merry Christmas" texts can fill the space they once held.

Look around. Really look. See the faces, hear the laughter, take in the chaos and the clinking glasses. Appreciate the people sitting beside you, because you never know which Christmas will be their last at that table. These are the moments, the memories, the tapestry we get to keep long after the guests are gone.

So, show up, wholeheartedly, while you can. In the end, the only gift that matters isn't under the tree, it's the people around it. If you can't manage that? Don't be surprised if the only present waiting for you *next year* is you pencilled in as a chapter of my next book, *Unwrapped: The People Who Didn't Show Up.*

Lesson: No Cash, No Presents, Just the Truth

Christmas isn't a transaction, it's a tapestry. Every laugh, every toast, every moment of genuine presence is a thread that binds us to our tribe. When people treat it like a pickup window, they don't just miss a dinner they leave a gap that weakens the whole fabric. The truth is, the only gifts worth anything are the people around the table. Show up for them. Cherish them. Because one day, those chairs won't all be filled, and the only thing left will be the memories we bothered to weave together.

Exercises to Complete

- **The Empty Chair Drill**
  Picture your Christmas table. Whose chair is empty someone gone, someone absent, someone you ache for? Write one memory with them that still makes you smile. Then jot down one way you can honour them this year.

- **Receipts vs. Relationships**
  List five "transactions" you've done out of obligation (gifts, cash, favours). Then list five genuine connections that cost nothing. Which list actually matters? Bet you, it isn't the one from Myer.

- **The Wake-Up Call Letter**
  Write an unfiltered letter (you don't have to send it) to someone who treated Christmas like a drive-through. Be honest, be fierce, be funny. Better out on paper than festering inside.

Take 5 – Checklist

- **Close the Window**
  Stop handing out love and leftovers through the emotional drive-through. If they can't show up, the window's closed.

- **Redefine "Nice List"**
  Reserve your gifts—time, energy, and presents—for people who actually make the effort to be there.

- **Redistribute with Joy**
  Pass unclaimed gifts to those who *do* show up (or keep them for yourself). Self-appreciation is tax-free.

- **Drop the Chase**
  No more begging for attention or reminders to call. Connection should never require a GPS tracker.

- **Weave Your Legacy**
  Keep stitching the tapestry your way. Every shared meal, laugh, or glass raised adds another golden thread of love—messy, beautiful, and entirely yours.

Quote of Choice

"Presence is the only present that matters." — Unknown

(And honestly, that's it. Presence is the only present that matters.)

CHAPTER EIGHT

Because the magic of Christmas isn't worth the migraine, or is it?

When everyone's too busy unwrapping gifts or devouring the trifle to notice the effort, you wonder: *What would happen if I just stopped?* If I didn't make the magic happen would anyone care, or even notice? What if I didn't chew up carrots and spit them onto the veranda to prove the reindeer had popped by? What if the garden wasn't sprinkled with Santa's footprints this year, or the jingle bells I shake just before bedtime went silent? Would anyone notice the reindeer skipped their snack or would they just assume they were on some low-carb, carrot-free diet this year?

What if I stopped painstakingly labelling presents in Santa's handwriting, making sure the tags looked rushed, as though scribbled at the North Pole? Would the kids still marvel at the magic or finally clock that Santa had the exact same stationery set as me?

I nearly got caught once. Nick, my eldest, was about eight old enough to start spotting the loose threads that could unravel the entire fantasy. It was Christmas morning, and as the kids tore into their presents, I was basking in the glow of their excitement, sipping tea (with a tot of Baileys for festive stamina), feeling like Santa's exhausted but triumphant assistant.

Then Nick froze mid-rip, holding up a gift tag. Brow furrowed, he asked, "Mum... why does Santa use the same wrapping paper as you?"

I froze too. My brain went into full-blown crisis mode, flipping through excuses faster than a dodgy magician riffling a deck of cards. *He borrows it from me! We're in a wrapping paper subscription service together! Australia Post delivered his paper to my house by mistake! Maybe Mrs. Claus forgot to do the shopping? Or the elves threw a Christmas rave and used it all up? Or...or...Rudolph ate it?* My inner monologue was spiralling. *It only looks like my paper, it's actually enchanted to blend in! Santa's wrapping paper magically changes to match each house! Maybe Santa just really likes my taste... because, let's be honest, I've got good taste in wrapping paper.*

Instead of any of those dazzling explanations, what actually came tumbling out of my mouth was the least convincing option of all: "Santa is very eco-friendly. He recycles."

Nick squinted, clearly suspicious but not quite ready to dismantle the magic. "Eco-friendly?" I nodded so vigorously I nearly spilled my Baileys, then launched into an unnecessary lecture about global warming and the North Pole's dwindling resources. It worked for the moment but I could see the seed of doubt had been planted.

From that day on, I knew I had to up my game. Santa got his own wrapping paper hidden deep in the closet, quarantined like it was 2020 and COVID all over again. I wasn't taking any chances. It was sealed off from the family stash like a potential biohazard, double-bagged and stored in isolation, just in case anyone got curious. If there'd been a government press conference about it, I'd have been there with charts and hand sanitizer, explaining "the measures we're taking to maintain Christmas integrity." I even bought a separate roll of tags and invented an entirely new handwriting style just for him, because when you're protecting the illusion, you go full containment protocol.

Let me tell you shaky left-handed scrawl at 1 a.m. after too much mulled wine is not as easy as it sounds. One year it looked whimsical, the next year it looked like Santa had been electrocuted mid-signature. Maybe it was the wine, maybe it was the sheer exhaustion, or maybe my creative genius just peaked at different times. Who knows? All I knew was that I was now running a full-blown forgery operation in the name of childhood wonder.

Keeping the magic alive is an endless cycle of lies and cover-ups wrapped in a bow. (Suspiciously similar to my next relationship, but don't worry, we'll spill that eggnog later.) The lengths we go to just to keep the illusion intact would put international spies to shame. Alternate handwriting styles, late-night missions in the garden, props and evidence carefully staged to withstand cross-examination by children who suddenly turn into forensic investigators the moment Santa is involved.

The hilarious part? The kids probably don't even remember that year. To them it was just another Christmas morning, another flurry of paper and squeals of excitement. But me? I'm still traumatised. I break into a cold sweat every time I see a roll of wrapping paper that even vaguely resembles the one I used that year. My pulse quickens, and I mutter under my breath like someone with full-blown festive PTSD: *Not this time, Santa. Not this time.*

However, the real circus begins with the presents themselves. Not just buying them, but trying to conjure up that mythical creature known as *the perfect gift.* The one that says, *I've been listening all year,* and *I know you better than you know yourself.* It's not gift-giving—it's emotional espionage.

The real problem? Half the people on your list already own everything, and the other half are "minimalists," which is code for "I don't want anything, but if you take that literally, you'll look like a heartless Grinch. So, you spend hours decoding cryptic wish lists, googling "what to buy for the person who has everything," and wandering through shopping centres in a trance, clutching novelty socks and overpriced candles because your brain has officially fried.

The pressure is relentless. Every gift feels like a test you're destined to fail: too practical and it's boring, too extravagant and you're showing off, too random and they'll quietly re-gift it at the next office Secret Santa.

That's before you even hit the traffic. Shopping in December isn't so much a retail experience as it is an endurance test. The car parks are full, the tempers are short, and the air smells faintly of desperation. You circle the same row seventeen times like a festive shark, silently praying someone will vacate a spot before you lose your Christmas spirit entirely. Inside, it's worse crowds moving at glacial speed, Mariah Carey is on loop, and you are walking behind that one person who insists on stopping mid-aisle to compare hand soap as if the fate of the nation depends on it.

Being clever (or so I thought), I once tried shopping early. The plan was flawless: glide smugly into December, mulled wine in hand, while the disorganised masses panicked and clawed their way over to the last Barbie Dreamhouse or PlayStation controller. I pictured myself serene and untouchable, like one of those mythical people who claim to have "finished Christmas shopping by September."

Reality? Very different.

Wow, I thought. *That can't be it.* It looked... sparse. Like the kind of gift pile that says, "We've fallen on hard times," instead of "I love you to the moon and back." No... worse. I was about to look like the Grinch. How had this happened? I thought I had it covered. I thought I was one of those smug, organised people who breeze through Christmas with serene smiles and perfectly wrapped presents stacked by December 1st.

Obviously not.

Panic set in immediately. Off I went—straight back into the thick of it all, into the last-minute shopping frenzy I'd sworn I'd never be part of. Elbow to elbow with the frantic masses, circling the shelves in a daze, grabbing whatever scraps were left. I was right back where I started, only sweatier, crankier, and significantly more broke.

Cut to months later, and I was unearthing rogue presents stuffed into wardrobes, wedged behind couches, or hidden in "genius" spots that only Past Me knew about, and Present Me had absolutely no hope of recalling. Every discovery felt like an archaeological dig into my own misguided efficiency. There I was, covered in sweat and regret, holding up a forgotten gift like, *Ah yes, a relic from the Great Panic of December.*

One year, I uncovered an entire stash in April. Brand new, still wrapped, still labelled, laughing from beneath a pile of winter jumpers. The sight was both triumphant and humiliating. On the bright side, birthdays were officially sorted. The downside? Everything was still in reindeer paper. Try explaining to a kid why their birthday present looked like it had just parachuted in from the North Pole. Soz for the kids with the Birthday closest to Christmas. They get the leftovers!

On paper, it looks like organisation. In reality, it's just self-sabotage. I'd start in November feeling smug and end up in April unearthing evidence of my own Incompetence.

But here's the million-dollar question: is the magic worth the migraine? The sleepless nights, the endless wrapping, the panicked realisation that you forgot batteries for the "must-have" toy now sitting lifeless under the tree. Is it worth assembling a bike at 2 a.m. with instructions that might as well be written in hieroglyphics? Is it worth sweating over Santa's handwriting, praying no one notices it looks suspiciously like yours after a bottle of Shiraz?

Yes. Why? Because the magic is the point. Not the money, not the prestige, not the perfectly curated tree or the expensive gifts stacked beneath it. It's the moments that shimmer, brief as fireflies and just as enchanting. The way children's eyes widen in wonder, as though they've just glimpsed the edge of another world. The hushed gasp when the first present is opened. The wide-eyed belief that reindeer really did nibble on carrots in the garden. The soft giggles that ripple through the house over something so small, yet so unforgettable.

That's what we're chasing. Those flashes of wonder that make time slow, that fill a room with light brighter than any fairy string. We weave the rituals, the late nights, the endless wrapping not for the gifts themselves, but for the way magic seems to brush past us when we least expect it. A giggle, a gasp, a sleepy smile at the end of the night, all little sparks that remind us why we do this dance year after year.

Yes, it's fleeting. It's gone as quickly as it comes, a shimmer, a spark, a blink between the noise and the silence. But in that instant, it's everything. The kind of moment that slips through your fingers but somehow stays pressed against your heart. It's the memory that will glow. Not in a blinding, fireworks kind of way, but in that slow, steady burn that lingers. Soft enough to soothe, strong enough to last, gentler than candlelight and warmer than mulled wine, the quiet after the chaos, the deep exhale after the storm. It's the warmth that settles in your bones, the kind that has nothing to do with the fire and everything to do with love.

So, when the next Christmas comes, we don't even question it. We dive back in, headfirst into the ribbons and rituals, chasing those sparks of wonder because even in chaos, the magic is what lingers and the magic is *always*, always worth it.

Lesson Learned: Is the Magic Worth the Migraine?

We pour our time, energy, and sanity into creating the "perfect" Christmas. From late-night toy assembly to traffic jams that feel like the end of days, the season can push even the most patient among us to the brink. But hidden inside the chaos are those fleeting, luminous moments of magic—wide-eyed wonder, bursts of laughter, a hush of joy that makes the madness fade. This chapter is about balance: holding onto the sparkle while letting go of the pointless pressure.

Exercises to Complete

- **The Gasp of Wonder**
  Think back to a moment when your efforts truly paid off, a child's squeal

of delight, a laugh that shook the room, or that quiet, knowing smile from someone who realised how much love went into what you did. Remember that instant when all the exhaustion, the wrapping paper cuts, and the near meltdowns melted away, replaced by pure joy. Write it down. Let it live somewhere you can see it—a note, a photo, a sentence. Because that moment, that spark of wonder, is why you do it. It's proof that the magic still works.

- **Find the Stress Spark**
  Pinpoint the one task that always makes you mutter, "Why do I do this to myself?"—wrapping, cooking, assembling bikes at 2 a.m. Now decide how you'll simplify it, skip it, or outsource it this year.

- **Define Your Magic Moment**
  What's the one thing that makes Christmas feel magical for *you*? Maybe it's a certain song that plays and suddenly the world feels softer, or that first quiet coffee before the chaos begins. Whatever it is, write it down. Name it. Protect it. That's your north star in the madness. Let everything else, the noise, the perfection, the pressure, fade into the background where it belongs.

Take 5 – Checklist

- **Pause for the Glow**
  Take five seconds to *feel* the moment—the laughter, the warmth, the chaos. That's the real gift.

- **Prioritise the Joy Spark**
  Choose one magical moment to create this year. Pour your energy there. Let the rest go.

- **Simplify the Chaos**
  Pick one task to scale back or ditch completely. (Example: no more car

park combat shop online and click "add to cart" instead.)

- **Cancel the Crisis**
  When something goes wrong (and it will), ask yourself: will this matter in an hour? If not, pour another drink and carry on.

- **Celebrate the Gasp**
  When someone lights up because of something you did, freeze that memory. That's the snapshot worth keeping.

Quote of Choice

"Christmas magic is silent. You don't hear it—you feel it. You know it. You believe it." — Kevin Alan Milne

(And sometimes, Christmas magic is hidden in the details we almost overlook, the small glance, a tiny squeal, the warmth of a hand on ours.)

CHAPTER NINE

The Invisible Woman of Christmas and the Fragile Baubles

I t's a paradox: the very acts that make Christmas magical are the ones that render women invisible. The tree doesn't decorate itself; the meals don't cook themselves; the gifts don't wrap themselves, yet society acts as if the holiday simply materialises overnight, conjured by some unseen force. And in a way, it is. That force is women, expected to embody selflessness, joy, and perfection all at once. Their labour is dismissed as "just what you do," rather than recognised as the extraordinary effort it truly is.

Invisibility at Christmas isn't just about being overlooked; it's about the quiet erasure of the person behind the role. When women are reduced to givers, nurturers, and doers, their own needs are buried beneath the weight of everyone else's expectations. And so, the holiday becomes less about celebration and more about obligation a stage where women perform their roles without ever taking a bow.

For years, I convinced myself that was fine. I'd gracefully step aside, letting others take centre stage on Christmas Day, while I settled for the understudy role of Christmas Eve. The warm-up act, if you will. I told myself it was better this way. After all, the kid's dad Trevor (He who cannot be named) had family here, and the kids needed to fit into their cousins' big family plans. I reasoned it wasn't about me it was about them. So I handed over Christmas Day like it was a neutral trade-off, pretending I didn't mind being the consolation prize.

I told myself it was selfless, practical, "for the kids." But deep down, it stung. I'd watch them go, bundled up with gifts, their faces lit with excitement, while I stood at the door, waving like a one-woman cheering squad. *Have fun!* I'd call, swallowing the lump in my throat as they disappeared into a day I wouldn't be part of. It wasn't jealousy. It was the ache of not being enough for the "real" Christmas. It was the reminder of failure.

So, Christmas Day became my leftovers. A day to "relax," I told myself. But let's be honest: I didn't want relaxation. I wanted noise. I wanted a pool full of kids, adults talking too loud, and inappropriate jokes flying across the table. Me relax Phaaaa! I have ADHD I do not relax, that is pure torture!

Perhaps the greatest irony is that invisibility isn't always imposed; sometimes, it's self-inflicted. We disappear by degrees. Women, in particular, have been expertly conditioned to equate love with labour, to believe that our worthiness lies in how much we give, how gracefully we juggle, and how seamlessly we hold it all together while pretending it's effortless. In that endless pursuit of creating magic for others, we risk vanishing altogether. It's a dangerous kind of disappearance, disguised as devotion. The more we give, the less of us seems to remain. We forget that we were supposed to *be in* the moment, not just *manage* it.

Yet, sometimes invisibility comes with unexpected perks.

Take, for instance, the years I perfected the art of being an invisible girlfriend. It wasn't intentional at first, I tiptoed into another relationship a foolish attempt at filling the Paul-shaped void. But what I really did was quietly fold myself down to fit someone else's shape.

Invisibility, as it turns out, has its benefits. It sneaks up on you in the strangest ways. You tell yourself it's peace—no fights, no drama, no tears by the tree. Just... calm. But it's not calm; it's erasure. I was so invisible in that relationship I wasn't even dumped on Christmas. Oh no, I made it through multiple Christmases completely unscathed. No dramatic exits, no scenes, no awkward gift returns at Boxing Day sales. Why? Because I was cloaked. Camouflaged. Hidden beneath his needs, his priorities, his delicate ego. I became the background music to his main event. I agreed when I wanted to object. I smiled when I wanted to scream. I became the woman who "didn't make a fuss," (most of the time – okay even ghosts make an appearance once in a while!) who "understood," who "knew her place." The truth was, I'd become so good at being invisible that even I stopped noticing myself. I stopped believing in myself. I blended in so seamlessly, I may as well have been a piece of festive décor a strand of tinsel, a bauble tucked at the back of the tree. Worthless.

Baubles. That's what he called them once – baubles. I was hanging them on the tree, carefully balancing glass on fragile branches, while he sat nearby like some armchair philosopher who'd spent too much time on Google swirling his wine and waxing lyrical about the "delicate nature of a man's pride" and how women should build it.

"You have to handle it with care," he said, voice heavy with self-importance, "or it'll shatter."

At the time, I nodded along, balancing ornaments in one hand and my patience in the other. I'd learned that tone—that carefully measured agreement that keeps the peace while your soul quietly sighs. I realised he wasn't wrong, just not in the way he thought. Baubles *were* like his pride: delicate, hollow, and liable to smash into pieces at the slightest knock.

The thing about baubles, though, is they're all show. Sure, they're pretty to look at, but they're fragile, easy to shatter, and completely useless beyond their ability to hang on a branch and look shiny. His pride was as fragile and delicate as Christmas baubles, always teetering on the edge of shattering. Utterly exhausting to maintain. You couldn't challenge it, question it, or even look at it too long without risking a mess.

Yet, he seemed determined to test its limits, constantly throwing those baubles to the ground just to see how much they could take. Each fall left another crack, but instead of picking up the pieces, he'd blame the floor, the tree, or anything else in the room—never himself. It was a display both fascinating and exhausting, like watching someone juggle glass ornaments in a windstorm, while pretending the act isn't bound to end in shards. It was a delicate performance, a fragile dance of ego and denial.

Let's be real, most of the time, it's not the baubles being fragile. Baubles are fragile, we all know that. They're meant to be. That's part of their charm, their delicacy. But the real issue usually isn't the baubles; it's the tree they hang from. You can't expect even the strongest ornament to survive when the whole structure is tilting under its own instability. Some trees, some people, look solid enough from afar. Dressed up, well-lit, standing tall in the corner like they've got it all together. But get close, and you see it, the wobble. The crooked base. The quiet creak of something that's never really been secure. You hang your hope, your care, your love on that, and then act surprised when everything crashes down.

I took that invisibility skill set to the next level in that relationship. I wasn't just a girlfriend; I was a mirage 6 years in the making. A comforting presence in the corner, there to support, nurture, and never, *ever* ask for too much. I was the quiet understudy in his life's production, stepping in only when needed and fading into the shadows the moment the spotlight found him or I needed help. The charming leading man in a feel-good family drama where everything revolved around his storyline, complete with the carefully curated soundtrack of *his* favorite carols (because my playlist was "too sappy"). God forbid a woman enjoys *Silent Night* without being accused of emotional depth.

But the thing about being a comforting presence is that it's a one-way street. Comfort goes out, but it doesn't always come back. While he basked in the glow of his own spotlight, there I was, juggling emotional labor like a circus performer and wondering why no one thought to ask if I needed a moment to breathe—or a glass of wine, at the very least. Not a polite, "Would you like some wine?". A generous, therapist-approved, no-measuring-needed kind of pour. The kind that says, "You've held this show together, and you *also* deserve to sit down before the credits roll."

But that never happened. I was the one refilling everyone else's glasses.

Invisibility: it's a double-edged sword. Sure, it spares you the messy confrontations. But it also means you don't get seen at all. I wasn't ghosted I was preemptively evaporated. No notes, no closure, just a quiet fade into nothingness, like the faint echo of "Jingle Bells" long after the lights have gone down. For a long time, I told myself that was normal. Noble, even blend in, give everything, expect nothing. After all, hadn't that been my Christmas credo for years? *Be the magic, not the mess.*

The truth was crueller and simpler than any grand betrayal: he hadn't learned to love me, not yet, he'd said. "I'm getting there," he told me, as if love were a skill you could master with practice, or a gift you could unwrap later, once the timing was more convenient. Nearly six Christmases passed with that promise dangling like tinsel that never quite catches the light.

That admission stung sharper than any outright rejection. At least if someone hates you, there's clarity in it. But this? I was neither loved nor free. It was like being left off the Christmas list altogether not good enough to be celebrated, not bad enough to be cut loose. I became the stocking no one bothered to fill hanging there year after year, empty, waiting.

Being told he was "getting there" wasn't a gift it was a reminder that I was perpetually on lay-by, waiting to be claimed, never quite worth the ribbon or the bow. That left me hollow. Worse than rejected outright, I was the unwanted ornament not shiny enough to put on display, not broken enough to throw away. Just dangling quietly at the back of the tree, unseen.

That's when the scaffolding started to appear. He hadn't learned to notice the scaffolding the way it was slowly being erected around him, piece by piece. I was building supports he never saw, shoring up the cracks before they split wide open, tightening bolts so nothing collapsed. I kept building, tightening, reinforcing, until one day I realised the structure was so high it blocked me from view. That's when the scariest question surfaced: *If no one else sees me, do I even see myself?*

Answering that was far scarier than any Christmas drama I thought I'd avoided.

When I finally faced the truth, it wasn't rage that hit me, it was emptiness. The quiet heartbreak of realising I hadn't been forgotten with fireworks or slammed doors, but through neglect. I'd been the one pulling the sleigh while He sat back and enjoyed the ride. When *He* finally hopped off? He didn't even bother to wave.

So yes, *His* exit was quiet. Forgettable. But it left me with one unexpected gift: clarity. The realisation that invisibility only lasts as long as you allow it to. I'd been erased gently, like a smudge on a festive window wiped away when the decorations come down.

But here's the gift I claimed for myself: *If no one else sees me, I will see me. If no one else celebrates me, I'll celebrate myself.*

So, this year, if you're feeling unseen, remember this: it's not about their appreciation, it never really was. It's about your own recognition of you.

Your permission.

The quiet, defiant act of saying, *I matter too.*

Cook if you want to.

Clean if you must.

But do it because *you* chose to, not because it's expected.

While you're at it, pour yourself the first glass of champagne, the tall one, with the bubbles that giggle back at you. Take the best slice of trifle, the one with the good custard-to-cream ratio and eat it before anyone else even notices dessert's on the table.

The invisible woman of Christmas has done her time. She's smiled through exhaustion, made magic out of mayhem, and kept the peace when she should've been resting. So go on, dim the fairy lights, light your own spark, and toast yourself.

Lesson: The Invisible Woman of Christmas and the Fragile Baubles

Invisibility at Christmas can feel like a deep ache giving and giving while quietly being erased in the process. However, visibility starts with you. It's time to stop being the wallpaper that blends into the background and start being the centerpiece of your own holiday. This chapter is about prioritising your joy, celebrating yourself, and reclaiming the spotlight you deserve. Because if you don't celebrate you, who will?

Exercises to Complete

- **Your Holiday Highlight Reel**
  Write down one thing you absolutely love about yourself during the holidays. Maybe you're a brilliant gift wrapper, folding paper so crisply it could slice bread. Maybe you're the master storyteller who can spin the same family anecdote for the fifteenth year and still get laughs. Maybe you're the queen of festive playlists, knowing exactly when to slip in

Mariah without anyone rolling their eyes. Whatever your sparkle is, name it. Celebrate it. And most importantly slow down long enough to enjoy it instead of rushing past it on your way to the next chore.

- **The "No" List**

  Write down one obligation that leaves you drained or invisible. Maybe it's hosting the extended family feast single-handedly, baking enough cookies to feed a small army, or buying gifts for people who don't even send a thank-you text. Then decide: will you politely say "no" this year, or delegate it to someone else? Either way, free yourself from it. Because martyrdom doesn't make Christmas brighter—it just makes you tired.

- **Spotlight Statement**

  Write a short, proud statement about what makes you shine at Christmas. For example: *"I am the glue that holds this day together,"* or *"My thoughtfulness creates magic."* Say it out loud when invisibility creeps in—bonus points if you do it in the mirror with a glass of champagne. This is your affirmation, your truth, your permission slip to stop shrinking into the wallpaper and take up space as the centerpiece.

Take 5 – Checklist

- **Pour the First Glass**

  Whether it's champagne, cocoa, or tea, pour yourself the first drink of the day and toast to you.

- **Claim the Best**

  Take the best seat, the first slice, or the quietest moment. No waiting for permission—it's yours.

- **Celebrate Your Wins**

  Pause and reflect on one thing you've done to make Christmas meaningful. Let yourself feel proud.

- **Delegate or Ditch**

  Choose one task that erases you. Hand it off or drop it entirely.

- **Shine Your Light**

  Do one thing that makes you feel seen. Dress up, play your music, tell your story. Take centre stage.

Quote of Choice

"Don't let anyone dull your sparkle." — Unknown

(Even if they try, remember: the centerpiece always shines brightest when it's lit from within.)

CHAPTER TEN

Operation Santa Redemption

It was one of those parenting moments destined to go down in family history as both legendary and mildly disastrous. My cousin Debi brilliant, pragmatic Debi decided it was time to rip off the Band-Aid and tell her kids the truth about Santa. No sugarcoating, no half-truths, just the cold, hard facts: Santa wasn't real.

To her credit, she delivered it with all the sincerity of a TED Talk on life lessons. Feeling rather pleased with herself, she thought she'd done the right thing. No more lies, no more elaborate ruses involving half-eaten carrots and jingle bells in the dead of night. Debi even gave herself a metaphorical pat on the back for her honesty until she saw the looks on her kids' faces. Their wide-eyed wonder had been replaced with something far worse: Betrayal.

She told me how, she could almost hear their little hearts cracking as they processed the news. One of them even muttered, "So... you've been lying to us this whole time?" Ouch. That one landed like a lump of coal to the soul.

In that moment, Debi realized she hadn't just killed off Santa, she'd accidentally murdered the magic of Christmas.

At that realisation she stood there frozen, clutching the tinsel like it might double as a defibrillator for the situation. What could she say? "Yes, my darlings, Mummy has been fabricating an elaborate global conspiracy involving reindeer, elves, and time-zone manipulation for the past eight years...surprise!"

She said she tried to backpedal, to soften the blow, but it was too late. The damage was done.

Cue the panicked phone call to me, equal parts guilt and desperation. "What have I done?" she asked, her voice trembling like she'd just confessed to a crime against humanity.

I paused, horrified. "What have you done?" I echoed. "Debi, you've created a Christmas catastrophe! This is DEFCON-level festive disaster. Do you even realize the magnitude here? You haven't just told them Santa's not real you've assassinated the magic of Christmas!"

"It's bad, isn't it?" she whispered.

"Bad?" I said. "Debi, it's the stuff of seasonal nightmares! Right now your kids are probably questioning every magical thing they've ever believed in. The Tooth Fairy? Gone. The Easter Bunny? History. Next, they'll be asking if we faked the moon landing!"

That's when inspiration struck. Operation Santa Redemption was born a plan so elaborate even Santa himself would've been impressed.

We weren't just scribbling a letter and calling it a day.

Oh no. We pulled out all the stops: handwritten letters from Santa, follow-up calls (disguised voices included), and enough glitter to make the house look like the North Pole exploded.

Mission Title: "Operation Santa Redemption" — Execution Plan

Mission Statement: Conduct a controlled narrative operation to restore Christmas Magic and re-establish parental credibility by shaping perceptions, managing information, and consolidating goodwill with minimal collateral emotional damage.

Commander's Intent: Restore trust and pride in parental provision so that children reinterpret recent events as intentional, noble, and beneficial; leave the family unit stronger and more resilient.

High-Level Objectives

Information Correction: Deliver an authoritative message that re-frames Santa's absence as intentional and altruistic.

Perception Management: Shape child and extended-family perceptions so parents are seen as generous and self-sufficient rather than deceptive.

Morale Consolidation: Rebuild emotional security and family pride.

After-Action Stability: Ensure long-term narrative coherence and minimise recurrence of trust erosion.

Command & Control

Mission Commander: Parent-in-Charge (Debi/Terry)

PsyOps (Letter Team): Produce, authenticate, and deliver the Santa letter.

Logistics: Ensure gifts/presentation match the script (no mismatched reindeer paper).

Moral Support Unit: Provide comfort, answer questions, manage tears.

Media Relations (Family PR): Prep short lines for extended family if they query ("Santa's targeted efforts are amazing this year").

Risk Assessment & Mitigation

Risk: Narrative rejected (kids feel lied to).
Mitigation: Immediate empathic debrief; admit intent to protect and explain.

Risk: Extended family undermines message.
Mitigation: Coordinate family PR; brief key relatives in advance.

Risk: Over-complication (too many theatrics).
Mitigation: Keep the letter concise; anchor with one clear, believable reason.

Mission Phases

Phase 0 — Reconnaissance (INTEL PREP):

- Conduct soft intel: observe child emotional state, gauge family sentiment, identify likely secondary reactions.

- Map vulnerabilities (who will ask questions, who needs extra reassurance).

Phase 1 — Shaping (PSYOPS):

- Draft authoritative communique (the Santa letter) that reframes reality: Santa prioritises need.

- Tone: sincere, elevating, non-blaming.

- Approve messaging and rehearse delivery.

Phase 2 — Infiltration (DELIVERY):

- Insert message into family space (letter at breakfast, staged "from the North Pole" moment).

- Synchronise with small positive actions (unexpected treat, extra cuddle) to anchor the message emotionally.

Phase 3 — Main Effort (REBRANDING & CONSOLIDATION):

- Amplify narrative: stories that highlight parental generosity, examples of family abundance.

- Deploy visible symbolism (VIP-style "you're so lucky" framing, ceremonious unwrapping, small rituals that validate the new story).

Phase 4 — Exploitation (MORALE BOOST):

- Reinforce with follow-on actions: A special Santa call. Shared activity, one-on-one time, "special parent" moments.

- Monitor child responses and adjust tone/tempo.

Phase 5 — After Action / Stabilisation (AAR & GUARANTEE):

- Conduct debrief (age-appropriate) to process feelings.

- Establish durable rituals to anchor the new narrative (annual "We Provide" story, special note in stockings).

- Document lessons learned to prevent future incidents.

Essentially Santa had to set the record straight. And set it straight, he did. The letter explained that Debi had gotten it all wrong (poor Debi, bless her well-meaning but tragically misguided adult brain). Santa went on to explain he wasn't gone he was just working a little differently than *their mother* thought. He explained that he does not always visit every single house. He focuses on children who truly need him, the ones who might not have much under their tree without his help. That's why their house didn't get the full North Pole treatment anymore. Not because he didn't care, but because they were already so lucky and so loved by their parents that they didn't need his magic as much as other kids did.

Boom. Nailed it.

Suddenly, Debi and Terry weren't the parents who had murdered Christmas, they were going to be the superheroes who had out-Santa'd Santa himself. Ho, ho, holy crap, look what great parents they were going to look like. They were going to be the ones that provided so well, with so much love and abundance, that even Santa didn't need to bother.

Imagine it: the kids, wide-eyed and awestruck, processing the news not as betrayal but as prestige.

Legendary.

It was going to be in one glitter-dusted stroke, they were going to go from "you lied to us" to "wow... our parents are basically the VIP lounge of Christmas." They'll be proud, proud to be the children of such generous, selfless, mythical parents. The kind who provide so well, with so much love and abundance, that even Santa himself can clock out early, hang up his boots, and say, "You know what? They've got this one covered."

As for the **"confirmation call."** Jingles bells and all the rest, this was going to be hard hard evidence. Something stronger than glitter and suspiciously familiar handwriting. Later that evening, Santa himself "called" to confirm the letter's authenticity. Debi sat there, holding the phone out to her kids like it was the

Holy Grail of Christmas. On the other end, in "his" best deep, jolly voice, Santa chuckled: *"She sometimes forgets, but Christmas magic always finds a way."*

Nailed it.

Instant credibility.

The kids' jaws dropped.

Their eyes widened.

You could practically hear the sound of their tiny worlds being re-stitched back together. The betrayal was gone (or Shite – had we actually created it?), replaced with awe. Santa was actually phoning them at their house. Let's be honest, it was next-level parenting, too. This wasn't just damage control; this was a masterclass in festive PR. Forget North Pole operations—Debi and Terry had just launched their own high-stakes rebrand as *the parents who even Santa calls.* Parents *So* important, *So* on top of things, that Father Christmas himself had to check in personally. In that moment, they weren't just providers they were Christmas legends. The kind of parents kids brag about on the playground. "Oh, Santa left you a note? Cute. At my house, he actually calls." Mic drop.

For good measure we went back to the classics. We chewed carrots at midnight and spat them onto the veranda, stomped boot prints in the garden, and dusted a little flour by the fireplace for that snowy effect.

Operation Santa Redemption wasn't just a success it was a triumph. As I looked at Debi, now wearing a Santa hat and fully leaning into the act, I couldn't help but laugh. "You know," I told her, "This may be your greatest parenting fail and your greatest save. Welcome back to the magic."

From that day on, we vowed never to underestimate the power of a good story, a little glitter, and the resilience of Christmas magic.

So, if you ever find yourself in a Santa-related pickle, remember this: the magic isn't really about Santa at all it's about the innocence of children and their boundless capacity for wonder. It's in the stories we tell, the way we nurture belief in something bigger, something joyful, something extraordinary. Kids don't just believe in Santa; they believe in the impossible.

To them, reindeer can fly, Santa squeezes down chimneys (even in houses that don't have one – a minor architectural detail to ignore), and the world is brimming with miracles just waiting to be discovered.

In a world that so often feels heavy and cynical, maybe we adults could use a little more of that childlike wonder. To dream, to laugh until our sides hurt, to let ourselves believe, not because it's literally real, but because it makes life richer, brighter, and infinitely more joyful.

Lesson Learned: Operation Santa Redemption

The magic of Christmas isn't really about Santa or reindeer breaking the laws of aerodynamics—it's about holding onto that childlike wonder that insists extraordinary things *can* happen. Even when the world feels heavy and cynical, the innocence of children nudges us to find joy, dream big, and believe in something a little magical. Sometimes, believing in the impossible doesn't just make life bearable, it makes it extraordinary.

Exercises to Complete

- **Your Impossible Dream**
  Think back to a time when you believed in something magical as a child. Maybe it was Santa, the Tooth Fairy, or a secret world you swore existed at the back of your closet. Maybe you believed your bike could fly if you pedaled hard enough, or that wishes made on shooting stars actually came true. Remember how it felt to live in that headspace wide-eyed, certain the world was bigger and kinder than it looked. Now, ask yourself: where did that belief go? Write about how it felt to live with that sense of wonder and then brainstorm one way to invite it back. Maybe it's choosing to believe in good news before bad. Maybe it's daring to make a ridiculous wish and acting as if it *could* happen. Maybe it's just letting yourself dream without editing. (adulthood doesn't cancel magic, we just stop looking for it.)

- **Create a Magical Moment**
  Magic doesn't have to be grand it just has to make someone's day feel lighter, brighter, or more surprising. Plan a small spark of magic for yourself or someone else. It could be leaving a handwritten note in someone's pocket, wrapping up a silly little "just because" gift, or telling a bedtime story with sound effects and wild hand gestures. For yourself, it might be making a decadent cup of hot chocolate and sipping it

by candlelight like you're in your own Hallmark movie. Write down your plan—and then actually follow through. The real trick? Don't announce it, don't explain it. Let the magic be its own reward.

- **Believe in the Impossible**
  Write down one "impossible" thing you wish were true. Maybe it's flying reindeer, endless holiday cheer, or finally finding a shopping mall parking spot without circling for 40 minutes. Maybe it's something bigger, like world peace or a family Christmas without passive-aggressive comments. Once you've written it down, find a small way to bring a slice of that impossible dream into your reality. Can't have reindeer that fly? Hang a paper one from the ceiling and give it glittery wings. Want endless cheer? Blast your favorite ridiculous holiday song at top volume and dance around the living room like a maniac. As for world peace? Start small—buy coffee for the stranger behind you, hold the door open, or forgive the relative who still owes you a Christmas ham. Symbolic or silly, the point is the same: embody a little of the impossible and watch it change how the possible feels.

Take 5 – Checklist

- **Pause for Awe**
  Take five minutes to notice something magical a wide sky, the sound of children laughing, or the simple sparkle of holiday lights.

- **Tell a Story**
  Share a whimsical or funny story with someone. Let yourself revel in the joy of storytelling, even if it's absurd or completely impossible.

- **Do the Impossible (Symbolically)**
  Do something playful that feels magical sprinkle glitter on a letter, pile marshmallows on hot chocolate, or write a note to your future self.

- **Laugh Out Loud**

  Find a way to laugh today. Watch something silly, share a joke, or let yourself be goofy without apology.

- **Spark Wonder**

  Spend a few moments dreaming about something extraordinary. What would you do if you could make one impossible thing happen? Picture it vividly.

Quote of Choice

Those who don't believe in magic will never find it." – Roald Dahl

(So let yourself believe—even if it's only for the joy of the journey.)

CHAPTER ELEVEN

Grudges & Other Christmas Curses

Thoughtlessness and lack of care it's the silent pandemic of our time, spreading faster than a TikTok dance trend no one actually finishes learning. We live in an age where gratitude has been overshadowed by entitlement, where a grown man throwing a tantrum about being wished *Merry Christmas* last in a WhatsApp group feels perfectly justified.

Yes, that really happened. My friend Gez told me about the digital drama unfolding in her family chat group, where one "adult" (and I use that term loosely) decided to make Christmas all about his fragile ego. The crime? His mother dared to wish him Merry Christmas *after* she'd already wished extended family scattered across the globe Merry Christmas first. How dare she! Absolute outrage. The absolute audacity.

You could almost hear the collective gasp of the WhatsApp group as this grown man, presumably one with a mortgage and at least partial facial hair, had what can only be described as an emotional meltdown worthy of a rejected X-Factor contestant. His mother had committed the ultimate Christmas sin: not being first. The man was genuinely wounded, as though she'd handed out her love in strict order of importance.

Another case of those *Fragile Christmas Baubles,* so delicate, they crack under the faintest flicker of perceived neglect.

Yet, the same lack of care sometimes hits painfully close to home. While it's easy to roll our eyes at other people's festive theatrics, the tantrums, the WhatsApp wars, the fragile egos wrapped in tinsel, it's a lot harder when the mirror points back at you. Yeah, that is so much harder to swallow.

This past year how often did my own children call their 80-year-old grandmother? A handful of times, at best. Even then, it was usually because I'd guilt-tripped them into it with the emotional subtlety of a Hallmark villain.

Let's be real, some of them have had more romantic flings than they've made phone calls to their grandmother. That's not even an exaggeration; it's a statistic that should come with a warning label and a government inquiry.

The thing is, they love her. I know they do. But love, these days, has become lazy. It hides behind texts and emojis and the occasional "Hope you're good" that's fired off between scrolling and snacking. Real connection has become old-fashioned, like handwritten letters or phone calls that last longer than your attention span.

It's not just them, though. It's all of us. We've collectively outsourced care to convenience. We 'like' posts instead of showing up. We comment "so proud!" under a photo instead of making an actual call. We send heart emojis to replace the sound of our own voices and convince ourselves that's enough.

But it's not. Not when you're 80. Not ever.

Every missed call, every "I'll do it later," adds up. One day, the roles will reverse. We'll be the ones waiting for the phone to buzz, clinging to the hope that some-one, somewhere, still remembers that love isn't supposed to be convenient. It's supposed to be deliberate. It is a choice. It is a decision. It's supposed to cost something. Time, effort and thought.

That is a big sting. Realizing that the people we've raised to be kind, capable, and clever have also inherited a world where consideration is scheduled between notifications.

It's a sobering reminder that somewhere along the line, we stopped teaching that *love is a verb*. Not a feeling, not a hashtag, not something you declare once and assume will auto-renew every year. It is a *doing*.

Love is meant to move.

It's meant to pick up the phone, show up, lean in, write the card, send the message, wash the bloody dishes without being asked.

The truth that landed like a lump of coal in my own stocking. I hadn't just let them fail her, I had failed them. Not because they aren't good kids, they are, they're amazing in so many ways. But because I hadn't guided them enough toward the simple, instinctive gestures of care. The reaching out. The checking in. The quiet moments of thoughtfulness that mean more than anything.

Instead of filling their stockings with trinkets, I should have been filling their hearts with the one gift that outlasts all the rest: the ability to show up unconditionally. Dive in with both feet.

That year I asked her not to give them anything, because at that point it had just become an automatic renewal. I didn't want their calls to be polite thank-yous prompted by a wrapped gift. I wanted them to be genuine, unprompted moments of care. The kind of calls that say, *"I love you, I miss you, you matter,"* not just, *"thanks for the money."*

That decision came after Mum told me about Takesure a young man who helps my mum with odd jobs back in Zimbabwe. My homeland may have its challenges, but entitlement hasn't yet reached epidemic levels (though, let's be honest, there are always a few universal dickheads). My mum had given him $300. He cried. Not the polite, dab-your-eyes kind of tears, but real, gut-deep, can't-hold-it-back gratitude. To him, that gift wasn't about luxury it was about hope, dignity and recognition. It mattered. It was life-changing in a way many of us, swimming in our sea of excess, often forget. While people here drop hundreds on Boxing Day sales without blinking, for Takesure, that cash was a reminder that he was seen, valued, cared for, and it opened a new door for him.

That's the point, isn't it? Showing up.

Caring enough to reach out, not just when there's a gift involved, but in the moments when it matters most. It's the phone call to say "I love you," the effort to settle differences before they calcify into grudges, the willingness to bridge the silences and soften the edges of pride. So often, it isn't distance or circumstance that keeps us apart, it's the things we leave unsaid, the reaching out we never quite get around to doing.

That was the pain I felt for Courts. Watching her go through her banishment and blocking from the family WhatsApp group by the Bauble-Crusher-in-Chief?

No one.

No one reached out.

Not a single call, not even a half-hearted emoji.

Not a single person.

Just silence.

"Not a creature was stirring, not even a mouse."

She put on a brave face because that's who she is, but I am sure it stung. She too got the invisible, ghosting treatment, left to carry the weight of *"Silent Night"* while the so-called season of love and peace.

In the silence left by the Block-and-Banish Brigade, she became our gift. That very rejection handed us the gift of her presence. Instead of sitting alone, she sat with us. Instead of being pushed to the margins, she became a part of our table, our laughter, our day.

It was a gentle reminder that family isn't defined by bloodlines, but by presence. No glitter, no fake smiles, no carefully crafted excuses about "how busy things have been." No last-minute texts or half-hearted explanations. The kind of people who don't need to explain their love because it's already in the room with them. It was one of the most honest, joy-filled, and healing Christmases I've had in years.

For now, while she waits to be unblocked, Courtenay will keep doing what she does best, living, loving, being shockingly candid, and blessedly unbothered.

Those sitting on frosty Mount Crumpit, nursing grudges like they're priceless family heirlooms, well maybe one day, like the Grinch they'll finally pause long enough to hear the laughter echoing down below, the clinking of glasses, the warmth of people who chose joy over pride. In that echo, maybe they'll realise they were never shut out, they just locked themselves out. All it ever took was the courage to climb down, open the door, and grow a bigger heart.

You see, that's the thing, true love and connection can't be forced back into places that have no room for them. You can't squeeze warmth into a space that's gone cold, no matter how hard you knock or how many olive branches you wave. Sometimes, you must stop knocking altogether and just build yourself a new door. A door that opens to laughter, honesty, and people who want to step inside.

If one day, their hearts do grow three sizes, and they feel that tug of longing and decide to come down from their frosty perch, Courts will still have room at her table. Roast beast and all. Because forgiveness doesn't mean forgetting; it means keeping a seat open for when love decides to return, humble and hungry.

After all, even the Grinch didn't come back because he was begged he came back because he finally chose to see the beauty in what he'd been missing. Maybe they will too. Eventually. Maybe then they'll feel that small, uncomfortable tug, right in the centre of the chest where the heart should be. With time, and a little discomfort, they may realise that while they were busy clutching their grudges, life went on without them. That joy didn't pause, laughter didn't stop, and love didn't shrink to fit their absence. They'll see that connection was always there, alive and thriving, waiting for them to choose it.

The Grinch didn't return with a grand apology or a dramatic monologue, he simply showed up, a little late, a little humbled, and finally ready to belong. That's the beauty of it. No fireworks. No parade. Just a decision to let go of bitterness and reach for something warmer. When that happens, it may just be the most underrated Christmas miracle of them all.

Lesson Learned: Grudges & Other Christmas Curses

The greatest gift we can give isn't wrapped in ribbon—it's wrapped in time, attention, and the simple act of showing up. Gifts might dazzle for a moment, but presence lingers. It holds space, it builds memories, and it reminds us that what people need most isn't another scented candle, it's to be seen, heard, and held.

Exercises to Complete

- **Your Presence Inventory**
  Make a list of five people who truly value you for who you are. Not for what you give, not for what you do, but for simply being *you*. Think of the ones who light up when you walk into a room, who don't care if you brought wine or forgot dessert, who would rather have your company than any gift. Now, choose one of those people and carve out intentional time for them this week. Not rushed, not squeezed in between errands. Show up fully. No phone buzzing on the table, no half-listening while scrolling. No alarms. Just you, all in. Notice how different the moment feels when you give your undivided self, and notice how *seen* the other person feels too.

- **The No-Gift Challenge**
  Choose someone you'd normally buy a gift for and flip the script. Give them something money can't buy – your presence. Maybe it's an afternoon together, a handwritten letter that says the things you usually leave unsaid, or a walk where you leave your phone in your pocket but have your ears wide open. Pay attention to how it feels to give from the soul instead of the shopping centre. The beauty of this exercise isn't that it saves money (though it might), but that it shifts the focus from *stuff* to

substance. You'll likely find that what lingers far longer than a wrapped box is the memory of being loved in a way that can't be bought.

- **One-Hour Disconnect**

  This one sounds deceptively simple: give yourself (and those around you) the gift of undivided attention. Choose one hour this week—phones down, screens off, no multitasking. Be with someone, or even just yourself. If you're with another person, notice what happens when the constant digital hum disappears. If you're alone, notice what surfaces when you're not numbing out with noise. Write about how it felt. Was it awkward at first? Was it liberating to hear real conversation without notifications interrupting? Did peace creep in where distraction usually lives? Don't be surprised if the answer is "all of the above."

- **Memory Over Merchandise**

  Think back to a time when someone's presence meant more to you than any gift they could have bought. Maybe it was a friend who sat with you in silence when you were grieving, or a parent who came to your school play, or a partner who listened without judgment when you finally let it all spill out. Write about that memory in detail—what they did, how it made you feel, why it mattered. Then ask yourself: how can you offer that same kind of gift to someone else this season? Because no matter how many shopping bags we drag home, the moments that live in our bones are rarely about merchandise—they're about people who cared enough to show up.

Take 5 – Checklist

- **Put the Phone Down**

  Silence the noise literally. Step away from the screen and step into the moment.

- **Make Eye Contact**

  Yes, actual eye contact the thing we did before emojis. Let someone feel truly seen.

- **Ask, Then Listen**

  Ask someone how they're doing, and then really listen. Don't fix. Don't scroll. Just be there.

- **Say the Thing**

  Say what you've been holding back: *"I love you." "I appreciate you."* Say it now, not when you wish you had.

- **Be in the Room**

  Wherever you are, be all there. Not in next week's to-do list. Not in yesterday's regret. Just here.

Quote of Choice

"The best and most beautiful things in the world cannot be seen or even touched—they must be felt with the heart." - **Helen Keller**

(And sometimes, all it takes is your quiet, undistracted presence to remind someone they matter.)

CHAPTER TWELVE

COVID, Camping, and the Liquid Briefcase

I f you've ever wondered what hell looks like, let me paint you a picture. It's me, camping, lying in a stifling tent, sweating buckets from both the Australian summer and a raging COVID fever, wondering if I'm dying or if this is just what Christmas feels like now. No running water, no electricity, no Wi-Fi. Just me, my increasingly feverish brain, and the faint sound of someone else's holiday joy drifting through the air.

Why do I f*king hate Christmas? Let me count the ways, starting with this Christmas camping disaster.

Christmas, for most people, is twinkling lights and gingerbread-scented cheer. For me, it was a five-day fever playing out in a nylon oven, surrounded by nature that didn't care one bit about my misery. Birds chirped cheerfully while I lay there, too weak to even swat the mosquitoes dive-bombing my face like kamikaze pilots. It got so bad I started naming the mosquitoes. "Oh, you're back, Steve? Still working on that left ear? Tenacity's your strong suit." Fever delirium meets David Attenborough it was as festive as it sounds.

The air was thick enough to chew, the tent was radiating heat like a toaster, and my body was a human hotplate of delirium and self-pity. At one point, I was convinced the tent was actively trying to kill me. The flaps refused to open properly, trapping me in a humid cocoon of my own misery. I was sweating so much I could've solved the drought if someone had wrung me out. My only drinking water? Warm, an experience no one should endure twice.

Comfort? Just the occasional breeze reminding me what fresh air used to feel like and my own fevered thoughts for company. At one point, I hallucinated Santa waving at me from the corner of the tent. Turned out it was just a sock I'd forgotten to pack away.

Somewhere between the fever and the humidity, I started wondering if this was it. Was this how I'd go out: alone, sweaty, and muttering curses at Santas I seemed to be conjuring up. I am pretty sure, one was waving, another was shaking his head in disappointment, and I swear one of them mouthed, "You should've stayed home."

The true soul-crusher? The absence of Christmas spirit. No, not the "cheer" kind, I mean the *liquid* kind. My throat felt like I'd been gargling with broken glass. Even the thought of a sip of wine made me wince, which meant my usual coping mechanism for Christmas chaos was officially off the table.

Instead, I was stuck with rehydration drinks.

No mulled wine, no eggnog, no cheeky mid-afternoon bubbles. Just me, grimly clutching my Electrolyte like it was a cruel joke in a bottle. Christmas spirit? Ha. Please. The only spirit whispering to me was the one saying, *"You're not going to survive this."*

Meanwhile, somewhere out there, normal people were clinking champagne glasses under fairy lights, basking in the glow of air-conditioning. I could almost see their LED tree toppers mocking me from afar, calling me toward civilization, comfort, and the sweet relief of an actual bed. But there I was, trapped in my nylon dungeon, wondering if drowning in my own sweat was technically possible. (It's not. But it feels close.)

This wasn't just a bad Christmas. This was Christmas taking a personal grudge against me. "You think you've had bad holidays before? Hold your eggnog." It only got worse.

Let's not forget the "liquid briefcase" our affectionate name for the portable loo that six of us were forced to share. Christmas magic in a plastic box stuffed to the brim with everyone's digestive regrets. It was, on the one hand, a marvel of human ingenuity, and on the other, a cruel social experiment designed to test the limits of human endurance, nasal fortitude as well as Friendship.

Every visit to that claustrophobic cube was like playing a round of olfactory Russian roulette, you never knew which chamber would fire, but you knew it would be deadly. By day two, I was convinced it was holding onto more than just waste; it was harbouring grudges, fermenting evil, plotting its revenge. The heat only made things worse. The "briefcase" didn't just smell, it radiated a malevolent presence, as if it wanted to climb out and join us for Christmas lunch.

Opening that lid was like lifting the gates of hell: hot air rushed out, thick enough to chew, carrying with it the ghosts of Christmas dinners past. I swear I heard carols in there once, but not the cheerful kind more like the screams of doomed souls set to the tune of *Silent Night*.

The situation with the "liquid briefcase" got... urgent. We'd all been playing a dangerous game of avoidance, holding out as long as humanly possible rather than face its wrath. But eventually, the inevitable moment arrived. We'd reached what we dubbed "touching cloth" territory that vital point of no return when waiting is no longer an option and the grim reaper of digestion demands tribute.

There's a special kind of camaraderie forged in those moments when six grown adults are silently calculating whose bowels will break first. Forget Christmas carols, this was a choir of clenched butt cheeks and whispered prayers. The tension was so thick you could slice it with a butter knife, though God help you if the butter was involved. We sat there cross-legged, avoiding eye contact, each of us knowing that one more mouthful could be the final straw that tipped you over the edge.

If Santa ever needs humbling, I'll gift him a week with that thing. Forget the naughty list spend one evening perched on the throne of doom and you'll repent for every sin you've ever committed. *Ho, ho.... No!*

So, what did I learn from this Nightmare out Camping? That camping is not for me. That running water and electricity are far more magical than fairy lights. That a flushing loo deserves a standing ovation.

No! really what I learnt was that it is about picking yourself up, dusting yourself off, and laughing until your belly hurts. Because if you can't find the humour in a fevered tent of doom or a liquid briefcase of horrors, then what's the point? Life's messiest moments make the best stories and this book is proof.

Here's my challenge to you, Christmas: bring it on. Throw your worst at me your glitter-covered chaos, your turkey that won't cook evenly, your lights that tangle themselves like they've got something to prove because no matter what you throw, I'll untangle, I'll laugh, I'll cry (probably into a glass of wine), and then I'll beat you at your own game, all with my best friend cheering me on.

That trip proved something no liquid briefcase could flush away: there's a gift more powerful than fairy lights or eggnog, *sisterhood*. Sisterhood is the unbreakable bond that steadies us when everything else collapses. It's the laughter that slices through chaos like a lifeline, the collective strength that says, *"We've got this, and if we don't, we'll fake it till we do."*

That's exactly what Angie did for me that Christmas. While I lay there in my tent of doom, a sweaty, feverish mess, she showed up. No questions. No judgment. Just her steady, unwavering presence. She didn't care that I looked like an extra from a low-budget survival documentary, or that my conversational skills had shrivelled to those of a damp sponge *or* even that she might catch COVID. She just cared. She showed up with a plate of food in one hand and a damp cloth in the other, like some kind of Christmas Fairy Godmother.

Lesson Learned: COVID, Camping, and the Liquid Briefcase

Life throws curveballs, but it's how we catch (or artfully dodge) them that shapes us. My disastrous COVID Christmas wasn't just a series of unfortunate events—it was a sweaty, fevered reminder that even in the middle of chaos, humor and sisterhood can shine through. This chapter is about survival, not just in a tent of doom, but in life's most ridiculous and challenging moments the best response is to laugh, dust yourself off, and lean on the people who show up, or be that Christmas Fairy Godmother and show up for someone.

Exercises to Complete

- **Find the Funny in the Frustration**

  Think of a time when everything seemed to go spectacularly wrong the meal burnt, the relatives argued, the weather sabotaged your plans. Write down the most absurd or comical details. What made it ridiculous in hindsight? Did it feel like the universe was pranking you? (Bonus points if it involved your own "liquid briefcase" moment) Recognise it as the kind of chaos that's awful at the time but pure comedy gold later. The goal isn't to relive the pain, but to find the humour and laughter hiding in the disaster.

- **Your Sisterhood Story**

  Think of someone who showed up for you when you needed it most. Maybe they sat beside you in silence, brought food without asking, or simply reminded you that you weren't alone. Write them a thank-you note or message even if you never send it. What did their presence mean in that moment? How did it shift the weight you were carrying? And how can you pay that forward by showing up for someone else this season?

- **The Reindeer Poop Challenge**

  Every Christmas comes with its own version of reindeer poop—the stuff you don't ask for but inevitably lands in your lap. Maybe it's tangled lights that tie themselves into sailor's knots. Maybe it's family drama that explodes like clockwork. Maybe it's the turkey that *never* cooks evenly, no matter how many YouTube tutorials you follow. Pick your personal "reindeer poop" and, instead of stewing in frustration, turn it into a dare. If Christmas is going to throw it at you anyway, how can you flip the script, laugh at it, and claim it as your own ridiculous holiday war story?

- **Bonus Option – The Tent of Doom Drill**
  Think of one situation you'd normally dread at Christmas hosting a meal, facing awkward relatives, enduring the chaos of travel. Now imagine you're back in my "tent of doom." Suddenly, that stress might not look so terrifying after all. Write down what you're dreading, then reframe it with humour: how could you exaggerate it into a story that's more funny than fearful? (If nothing else, it might give you material for next year's survival guide.)

Take 5 – Checklist

- **Pause and Laugh**
  Find the humor in the chaos. Even if it's just the absurdity of life reminding you that perfection is overrated.

- **Acknowledge Your Strength**
  You survived whether it was COVID in a tent or a burnt turkey. Own it. Give yourself credit where it's due.

- **Call Your Angie**
  Reach out to the friend who always shows up. Let them know they matter.

- **Reclaim Your Magic**
  Do one thing that brings you joy even in the madness. No glitter required.

- **Challenge the Chaos**

  Pick one of your "Christmas war stories" and wear it like a badge of honor. Survival is its own kind of magic.

Quote of Choice

"Maybe Christmas doesn't come from a store. Maybe Christmas... perhaps... means a little bit more!" – **Dr. Seuss,** *How the Grinch Stole Christmas*

(And honestly, if the Grinch really wanted to do me a favour that year, he could've skipped the presents entirely and just stolen the liquid briefcase.)

CHAPTER THIRTEEN

Because Perfection Is Overrated, and So Is Boxing Day

Boxing Day Madness—the one day of the year when Christmas joy gives way to sheer chaos, and the spirit of giving is replaced by the spirit of grabbing. People who just yesterday were singing about peace on Earth are now elbowing each other out of the way to claim their discounted prize.

Let's take a moment to marvel at the sheer absurdity of it all. You've just spent weeks, maybe months meticulously planning and shopping for Christmas. You probably spent hours deciding which gift to buy, comparing price tags and reviews like your life depended on it. You've wrapped gifts, stuffed stockings, and maxed out your credit card to build a mountain of festive cheer under the tree. Then, less than 24 hours later, before the gravy has even congealed you're sprinting to the mall and elbowing someone's grandma to snag the last discounted blender.

It's madness, pure, glitter-coated madness.

A frenzy.

Fully grown adults charging through aisles as if nabbing a half-price flatscreen is the key to survival. The pushing, the shoving, the arguments over who saw it first. All for things they didn't even know they needed until the word *SALE* flashed in front of their glazed-over eyes.

Oh, the glorious absurdity of holiday sales. Perfectly rational, functional humans suddenly lose their collective minds over things they neither want nor need. It's as if the word *SALE* flicks a switch deep in the lizard brain, triggering an ancient instinct to hunt, gather, and defend territory, but except instead of mammoths, it's discounted air fryers and electric foot spas.

"It's 70% off!" we cry, as if saving money on something we didn't plan to buy is a heroic act of financial strategy. Before you know it, you're proudly clutching your third toaster, a novelty popcorn machine, and a sequined jumpsuit that screams *Vegas Elvis* but whispers *closet regret*. But we justify it nonetheless *it was on sale! I saved money!* Saving money on something you never needed is like celebrating because you only set fire to $20 instead of $50. The math doesn't check out.

There's a special kind of delirium in those fluorescent-lit aisles. No one wakes up thinking, *You know what's missing in my life? A bacon-scented candle.* But slap a 30% discount sticker on it, and suddenly it's in the cart because, "Well, you never know when the house might need to smell like breakfast."

Holiday sales feed on a twisted kind of logic—they convince us that *not* buying something is the real mistake. You walk in thinking you're saving money, but somehow walk out with a blender, a bathrobe, and a mild sense of shame. It's retail witchcraft at its finest. We spend December swimming through a sea of stuff, clutching bargains only to realise half of it will end up shoved in the back of a closet—forgotten faster than a New Year's resolution at a bottomless brunch.

Buyer's regret is the hangover that follows the emotional migraine, kicking in somewhere between ripping off the price tag and realising you have absolutely no idea why you bought it. It's like waking up after a wild night, except instead of tequila shots and questionable texts, you're staring at a $200 air fryer wondering how it ended up in your kitchen when you don't even cook.

Sometimes the regret is instant like when your bank statement pings before the shopping bags are even unpacked. Other times, it sneaks up later, when the holiday lights are down and you're left alone with a novelty foot spa you once believed would "change your life." Yeah-Na: it won't.

Still, regret isn't entirely useless.

It's a ruthless teacher. It forces you to face the awkward truth, half your "holiday essentials" are clutter in a sparkly disguise. Did you really need that life-sized inflatable Santa? No! Did you really think a $200 throw would transform your home into a Better Homes & Gardens spread? Also, a big fat *NO!*

The worst part is the queues. Endless, soul-destroying queues. Lines of weary shoppers clutching their treasures like contestants in a bleak game show, while their children dangle from their arms like limp Christmas ornaments. Half the time, these so-called *"deals"* are nothing more than retailers offloading the same junk no one wanted before Christmas. The only difference is that the goods are now dressed up in neon stickers which say *Sale and scream Urgency.*

The audacity of it all. Take Lush, for example, where you are required to join the sacred Christmas Queue Experience, standing shoulder to shoulder with other weary pilgrims in search of fragrant salvation. You queue to get into the shop. You wait, sweating under fluorescent lights, inching forward like you're queuing for enlightenment, only to hand over half your grocery budget for a bar of soap shaped like a glitter-drenched polar bear. A queue. For soap.

Okay, fine, I'll admit it. I was there. The Boxing Day Sales. My personal walk of shame through fluorescent-lit chaos, clutching a special offers and my dignity, one of which didn't make it out alive. Shoulder to shoulder with Courtenay, shuffling forward like penguins on migration, silently wondering if a bath bomb could ever be worth this level of humiliation. Around us, staff bounced like caffeinated elves, brandishing handfuls of brightly coloured goop and promising it would make me smell like a meadow of unicorns. Meanwhile, my inner monologue was pure profanity—a running commentary of words that would have me permanently blacklisted from Santa's nice list. Not that it matters. Let's be honest, that sleigh sailed a long time ago.

It's capitalism at its most theatrical, whispering seductively, *"Yes, spend $24 to smell like a candy cane rolled in fairy dust. You deserve this illusion of self-care."* Then, just when you think you've escaped with your overpriced polar bear soap they hit you with *"If you spend just a little more—you'll get a limited edition ....!"* You do not even hear what it is you just say "*YES!*" You do not want to miss that one.

But when we think of it. Limited edition what, exactly? The only thing we get is another lump of a festive anxiety attack! But you have that soap shaped like a snowman's butt just to qualify and you end up walking out $87 poorer, reeking of synthetic peppermint, clutching a tiny pink cube of "bonus product" and somehow, against all logic, you still feel like you won.

Of course, there's always *that one friend* let's call her Andrea who takes it to Olympic levels. She and her husband just bought their second...or third...or fourth house (I've lost count), but she insists she needs to hit the sales for "essentials." Essentials like a $700 rug and a "statement lamp" that looks like something an octopus would wear to a gala.

Off she goes, hawk-eyed and laser focused. Five hours later, she emerges, battle-worn but triumphant, clutching treasures no one wanted in November but now, thanks to a *LIMITED TIME ONLY* sticker, are suddenly priceless. Proof that commercialism has won and that we're willing to elbow our dignity, our sanity, and our overdrafts just to play along. But why?

I can't even blame Andrea, not really. Because beneath all the madness, there's something painfully human about it. That tiny spark of emptiness we keep trying to fill with "just one more thing." The belief that happiness might be hiding inside a shopping bag, that contentment can be bought on clearance. That's what we're really chasing—not stuff, but the *lack of connection to people.*

The shopping, the sales, the chaos, it's all just a distraction from the ache of absence. It's easier to chase bargains than to sit still with what's missing. When we dive headfirst into retail therapy, it's not the lamp or the rug we're after, it's that feeling of connection, belonging, acceptance. The illusion that if we buy just one more thing, maybe we'll feel whole again.

But we don't need *more* to be enough, or to earn anyone's acceptance or approval. The people who matter already see our worth, even when we can't. We keep piling on layers, of stuff, of sparkle, of *"look how well I'm doing"* hoping they'll somehow cover the cracks that only love, time, and honesty can truly mend.

Somewhere along the line, we started confusing accumulation with affirmation.

We've told ourselves that if we look the part – successful, stylish, powerful - then maybe we'd finally feel worthy. But the shine always fades. The rug stains, the lamp dulls, and that fleeting rush of satisfaction evaporates as quickly as it came, leaving us right where we started, still searching for something real beneath all the gloss. .

This Boxing Day, here's the quiet invitation: remember that you are already enough, exactly as you are. The people who truly love you will love you through every mess, mistake, and unfiltered moment.

As for me? That's all I need to hear. Next year, I'm staying home. I'll be drinking espresso martinis for breakfast and laughing at all the suckers wrestling over discounted junk. Boxing

Day, consider yourself officially cancelled. Bottoms up, everyone.

Lesson Learned: Because Perfection Is Overrated, and So Is Boxing Day

Boxing Day sales are proof that we've turned Christmas from a celebration into a competition. The madness isn't about the blender or the bath bomb it's about the chase, the FOMO, the illusion that buying more somehow means *being more*. But the truth is this, no sale, no bargain, no neon discount sticker can compete with the real win time, laughter, and presence. Less really is more, and sanity is priceless.

Exercises to Complete

- **Your Boxing Day Confession**

  Write down the most ridiculous thing you've ever bought in a sale. Be brutally honest. Maybe it was the novelty popcorn machine, the life-size inflatable Santa, or the sequined jumpsuit you swore you'd wear to "all the parties" that never happened. Now, dig deeper: how quickly did buyer's regret hit? Was it the moment you saw your bank statement, or the moment you tried to justify it to yourself with, *"Well, it was 70% off"*? Reflect on what this says about your personal "SALE psychology." Are you driven by the thrill of the bargain, the fear of missing out, or the desperate hope that this one item will magically fix your life?

- **Swap Stuff for Story**

  Plan one experience you could give instead of a purchased gift. It doesn't have to be elaborate, sometimes the simplest gestures carry the most weight. A picnic in the park. A handwritten letter that says the things you usually keep unsaid. A long walk where the phones stay in your pockets. Or, for the truly brave, a night of bad karaoke where the memories are guaranteed to outlast the hangover. Now write about how it might feel for both you and the recipient. Would they even remember a novelty foot spa in six months? Probably not. But they'll remember the time you belted out "All I Want for Christmas Is You" badly enough to make the dog howl.

- **The 24-Hour Rule**

  Next time you feel the pull of a sale, pause. Don't grab it, don't swipe, don't click "buy now." Instead, write the item down and wait 24 hours. Then check in with yourself: does it still feel essential the next day, or has the adrenaline faded and left you wondering why you almost bought a third blender? This isn't about denying yourself joy, it's about separating joy from impulse. If, after 24 hours, you still want it and it still makes sense, fine. But if you look at the note and think, *"What was I even thinking?"* Congratulations, you've just saved money, cupboard space, and one more addition to the Clutter Hall of Fame.

Take 5 – Checklist

- **Step Away from the Cart**
  Before you hit "buy now," pause. Ask yourself if it's joy or FOMO driving this decision.

- **Shop Your Own Cupboards**
  Before adding to the pile, check what you already own. Chances are, your "new essential" is gathering dust somewhere.

- **Tell the Regret Story**
  Share one of your buyer's regret stories with a friend. Laugh about it. Shame loses its sting when it's funny.

- **Reframe the Win**
  Instead of "winning the deal," make connection your win. Choose time, conversation, or laughter as your trophy.

- **Celebrate the Escape**
  Skip one sale this season and celebrate your freedom with something indulgent—like espresso martinis for breakfast. (Cheers to sanity!)

Quote of Choice

"The quickest way to double your money is to fold it in half and put it back in your pocket." – Will Rogers

(Honestly, on Boxing Day, that might be the only real bargain worth grabbing.)

CHAPTER FOURTEEN

"Say Cheese, You Little Liars"

A h yes, the annual tradition of forced cheer and fabric-softener smiles: the Perfect Family Christmas Photo. A typical *authentic holiday joy* like spending 45 minutes threatening your children with the loss of Wi-Fi if they don't smile like their jaws aren't locked in repressed rage. That's before the dog pees on the matching tartan rug or Grandma yells something politically incorrect in the background.

You know the photos I mean. The whole family posed like a detergent commercial, beaming with the kind of joy that only comes from deep, simmering resentment and three takes too many. They are all over social media. Matching sweaters or shirts, freshly ironed (and steamed with someone's tears), kids smiling like they've just been bribed with iPads, and the dog staring directly into the void, reconsidering his contract with this family.

They're everywhere. They arrive in your inbox or mailbox wrapped in thick card stock and smugness. "*Warmest wishes from the Hendersons,*" it reads, beneath a photo so heavily filtered it belongs in the Louvre's Hall of Delusion. The parents look ten years younger, the kids are suddenly model citizens, and everyone's skin glows like they've been kissed by angels.

I get it. There's a part of me that wants to be that organised. I marvel at anyone who can get four humans and a dog looking in the same direction without tears. But mostly, I'm torn between admiration and the overwhelming urge to vomit into a sequin-covered gift bag. I know how the sausage is made: the stress, the yelling, the 347 rejected shots, the meltdown over the one sweater that arrived in "Satanic Scarlet" instead of "Noel Berry." Yet the final product looks effortless. Magical. Fake as tinsel on a cactus.

What have we done? We've traded stories by the fire for selfies by the tree, and then we wonder why Christmas feels so cold, even in the blistering heat of an Australian summer.

We've convinced ourselves the most loving thing we can do at Christmas is stage a lie to send to everyone we've ever met. Perfectionism, dipped in passive-aggression and wrapped with a bow. The photo screams, "We've got it all together," but the hidden caption might as well read: *"emotional blackmail in festive jumpers."* Merry Christmas everyone. Why is it so important to curate these lies?

We're told Christmas is about giving, but it seems these days to be about getting. Getting the best photo, the most likes, the loudest reaction. You know what's missing? Actual joy. Real smiles. The kind you don't have to bribe. You want a real Christmas card? Send the one where your youngest is mid-meltdown because someone touched their gingerbread house, and your eldest is side-eyeing like they could melt tinsel. That's the one I want on my fridge.

Because the truth is, a perfect photo doesn't prove you have a perfect life. It proves you know how to curate chaos and hide the mess. You've airbrushed the arguments, cropped out the exhaustion, and slapped a filter over the tears. But Christmas was never meant to be about hiding. Maybe it's about letting people *in*—into your real life, your real family, your gloriously messy, unfiltered story, just as we are.

So, here's to the outtakes: the wrinkled jumpers, the awkward poses, the chocolate-stained grins, and the blurry laughter shots. That's real. That's the magic. That's Christmas.

Lesson Learned: "Say Cheese, You Little Liars"

Joy isn't a staged smile. Real connection lives in the outtakes the chaos, the chocolate smears, the side-eye worthy of an Oscar. This chapter is about ditching the glossy façade and embracing the real, the raw, and the ridiculous. That's where the magic actually hides.

Exercises to Complete

- **Find Your Outtakes**

  Dig through those old photo albums (or the digital graveyard that is your phone's camera roll) and hunt down the funniest, most chaotic Christmas shots you can find. The ones where the dog is mid-pee in the background, Grandma's asleep with her mouth open, or someone's crying because they didn't get the bigger slice of pudding. Don't hide them, frame them. Hang them proudly. That's your true holiday masterpiece; a gallery of chaos that deserves wall space more than any glossy fake smile ever will.

- **Holiday Photo Re-Do**

  This year, stage a deliberately ridiculous family photo. No ironing, no forced cheer, no teeth-whitening apps. Pull out mismatched pajamas, bed hair, silly props, and catch yourselves mid-laughter. Stick the baby in a saucepan if you must (they'll forgive you). Make this the tradition: the annual "honest" photo, where joy is real and nothing matches. It'll be the one your kids laugh about for decades, long after the matching-sweater pictures have yellowed in a drawer.

- **Send the Chaos**

  Ditch the glossy photo card this year. Instead, write a Christmas letter or email sharing one hilarious, unpolished story from your year. The flat tire on the way to Grandma's. The kid who flushed the Elf on the Shelf. The pavlova that collapsed like your willpower on Boxing Day. Be bold, be messy, be the anti-card. People don't need another staged snowflake font, they need to laugh, to feel seen, to know you're just as gloriously imperfect as they are.

Take 5 — Checklist

- **Laugh at the Worst**

  Find your most disastrous Christmas photo and cackle like it's the masterpiece it truly is.

- **Ditch the Uniform**

  Say no to matching outfits. No one needs to look like a choir of polyester elves.

- **Cheer the Messy**

  Compliment someone's chaotic, unfiltered holiday photo online. Real deserves applause.

- **Snap Mid-Mayhem**

  Take a photo in the middle of the chaos, not after you've staged the "perfect" scene.

- **Get in the Frame**

  Let yourself be in the photo—even if your hair is frizzy, your jumper stained, and your patience thin.

Quote of Choice

"Every perfect Christmas card hides at least three emotional breakdowns and one passive-aggressive comment about lighting." — **Probably Me**

(yip that's why I do not do it)

Chapter Fifteen

Reclaiming Christmas - Unwrapping the lies, tinsel, and guilt one ribbon at a time.

So, as you've probably gathered from the disasters lovingly catalogued in earlier chapters, I've had my fair share of Christmases where everything went spectacularly, hilariously wrong. From being dumped by the so-called "love of my life" to nearly *"losing my own"* (slightly dramatic, but let's go with it) in a tent of doom somewhere in the Australian wilderness, Christmas has never failed to leave its mark. Oh boy, did it ever leave its *Mark* on me – quite literally, my best present yet in human form. And that, dear reader, was the one time the season finally got it right. Yet, despite the chaos, the tears, and the occasional Boa Constrictor, there were always people who showed up.

Which begs the question: why do we, rational adults, mind you, heap so much pressure on ourselves to create the *perfect* Christmas.

Why is it a high-stakes competition for the best Instagram photo, the most elaborate meal, and the shiniest pile of presents. It's exhausting. If you've ever felt like you're the only one drowning in it, this book is here to remind you: you're not alone and you have permission to let it all go.

Surviving Christmas doesn't mean gritting your teeth and enduring it. It means letting go of the pressure to make everything perfect, giving yourself permission to pause, and focusing on what truly matters. It's about rediscovering the magic in the smallest things.

It's about taking back the holiday from commercialism, guilt, and crushing expectations. It's about redefining what Christmas means to *you*—not what it "should" look like, but what it feels like.

This book isn't a rant. It's a guide, a survival manual, a raw retelling that reminds us Christmas was never meant to be about perfection. It's about the moments that make you laugh, cry, and carry on. If you've ever felt like Christmas was a battle you had to fight, this year is your chance to win it back not with tinsel and bows, but with the freedom to celebrate in your own imperfect, glorious way.

Of course, this madness isn't new. Like any good fairytale, it started *a long, long time ago.* The Victorians, bless their industrious little hearts, were the ones who really turned Christmas into the grand production we know today. Before Queen Victoria's reign, Christmas was modest, more about reflection and simple gatherings than tinsel-draped chaos.

The Victorians also gave us Christmas cards, courtesy of Sir Henry Cole in 1843, a man so busy he accidentally invented an entire industry. Too swamped to write personal letters, he hired an artist to design a single festive card he could mass-produce and send to everyone at once. Just like that, the world's first socially acceptable form of "copy-paste" was born. The original card featured a family raising a glass of wine — scandalous for the time. Naturally, it was a hit.

Before long, people everywhere were sending these tiny rectangles of obligation, each one designed to say, *"I remembered you exist, please don't be offended I didn't call."* Here we are, 180 years later, still buying overpriced glitter-coated guilt notes to prove our seasonal goodwill. Henry Cole may have been trying to save time, but he inadvertently gave birth to a tradition that now costs us hours of signing, addressing, and licking envelopes, just so we can send out reminders that we're still polite enough to care.

Dickens then cemented the whole thing with *A Christmas Carol*, turning Scrooge into a cultural shorthand while Tiny Tim became the poster child of goodwill. The story that single-handedly turned guilt into a festive tradition. Written by Charles Dickens in 1843 (apparently everyone was inventing Christmas that year), it follows the grumpy miser Ebenezer Scrooge, who hates Christmas almost as much as I do, though his problem was more ghosts and less glitter.

Dickens' attempted to remind Victorian England, a society obsessed with factories, status, and questionable hygiene, that perhaps humanity could use a little kindness with its capitalism. He wanted people to see that generosity mattered more than profit, that compassion should count for something in a world choking on coal dust and social ladders. However, here we are, another century and a bit later, with fancier soap, better lighting, and Wi-Fi, still trying to learn the same lesson. Different century, same story: and still needing a few ghosts to remind us what really matters.

Fast-forward to the 20th century, when Coca-Cola doubled down on the myth and rebranded Santa Claus into a jolly, red-suited mascot of consumer cheer. Suddenly, Christmas is a marketing campaign with a sugar rush, complete with jingles, slogans, and a side of emotional manipulation.

Then comes the modern era, and honestly, we've outdone even the Victorians in festive absurdity. Don't even get me started on Elf on the Shelf, that modern little abomination terrorizing parents worldwide. Imagine pitching it to a Victorian: *"It's a doll that spies on your kids, and you have to move it every night to prove Santa's watching."* They'd have called for an exorcism. Yet here we are, setting 3 a.m. alarms to stage elaborate elf hijinks for Instagram likes, while our kids couldn't care less.

While the Victorians may have invented the spectacle, it's on us to decide how we want to play it. Every now and then, someone decides to take a... different approach.

That's my friend Adam, who reclaimed Christmas while single-handedly redefining festive rebellion. Tired of his kids' endless lists, eyerolls, and general Christmas entitlement, he snapped. His grand comeback? He filled their stockings with coal. Actual, honest-to-goodness lumps of it. He had the courage to do exactly what the old legends threatened.

It was his personal protest against the madness, part social experiment, part parenting performance art.

Picture it: the whole wholesome family sitting cross-legged in their pyjamas, the twinkling tree lights reflecting off their eager little faces. The kids, vibrating with anticipation, each clutching a sack that looked suspiciously industrial. Adam, poker-faced, announces that Santa's been doing some "serious auditing" this year, and unfortunately... the results weren't great.

They open their bags, expecting LEGO or gadgets or at least some lollies — and instead, out tumbles coal. Cold, black, dusty lumps of it. The kind of gift that would make even Scrooge proud.

There was silence.

Then outrage.

Then confusion.

Then laughter.

In that moment, he didn't just reclaim Christmas — he *redeemed* it.

Once the initial horror wore off, they realised Dad wasn't being cruel, or a complete Dickhead, he was being clever. He wanted to remind them that Christmas wasn't about ticking items off a wish list; it was about gratitude, humour, and maybe a small lesson in humility. The gifts came later, of course, he's not a monster, but for those few delicious minutes, Adam got to watch his kids learn what it means when the magic of Christmas doesn't arrive neatly packaged in glossy paper.

Thinking back to my childhood, it was the lead up, the anticipation and all the preparation that made it magical. Part of that was the fairy lights with their stubborn glass bulbs. Every year, Dad would haul them out, plug them in, and...nothing. Not a flicker. Cue the family huddle, checking each bulb like detectives on the case of the century. Hours later, when the guilty bulb was finally replaced, the moment of victory felt like Christmas morning itself. Who knew a single glowing bulb could deliver so much joy?

Those moments were about togetherness, patience, and the hilarity of trying (and the concern that we could not get them working). They were slow, deliberate, joyful in their simplicity. No frantic dashes to Bunnings, no easy replacement. Just family, fumbling and laughing their way into the season.

This year, I'm making a pact with myself: I'm going to do things differently. I'm giving myself permission to focus on what actually matters what makes me feel alive, connected, and at peace.

I'm going to pour the first glass of wine for myself, take the time to breathe, and even say "no" to things that don't serve me.

This year, I'm choosing joy over obligation, connection over consumerism, and memories over material things. Life's too short to spend Christmas stressed out and invisible. So, here's to doing it differently, messy, imperfect, and unapologetically *me*.

So, as I draw to a close on this book, I leave you with this: Christmas doesn't have to be perfect to be beautiful. It doesn't have to be grand or expensive or meticulously planned.

Whether your holiday was filled with laughter or quiet reflection, whether you found yourself surrounded by family or savoring solitude, I hope you find something to hold onto—something real. And if not? There's always another season, another moment, and another chance to find what truly makes your heart sing remembering "The best gifts are the ones we give ourselves: peace, joy, and the courage to let go of what doesn't serve us."

So let's lift our glasses in a toast to reclaiming Christmas on your own terms. Let it be messy. Let it be imperfect. Let it be yours. And if all else fails, remember — leftover Halloween candy makes an excellent stocking filler, and while glitter tends to stick to everything (and show up in all the wrong places), so does a good laugh.

Lesson Learned: Reclaiming Christmas - Unwrapping the lies, tinsel, and guilt one ribbon at a time.

Reclaiming Christmas isn't about doing it "right"; it's about doing it *your* way — whether that means putting coal in your kids' stockings to teach them a lesson, serving pancakes instead of pavlova, or spending the day in pyjamas with zero guilt and maximum carbs. Forget the Hallmark version with its snow-dusted perfection and emotionally available men in flannel. Create a Christmas that feels genuine, joyful, and unapologetically yours — whatever that looks like, I hope it gives you sparkles.

Exercises to Complete

- Find your Coal Moment
  Think of one Christmas tradition that makes you roll your eyes so hard they nearly jingle. Now flip it. Hate Secret Santa? Replace it with *Secret Compliments*. Tired of forced carols? Blast your favourite non-Christmas playlist instead. Your "coal moment" is whatever you do to reclaim your peace — with humour, not guilt.

- **Give "Coal" Gifts**
  This year, give one person a "coal" gift — something practical, funny, or symbolic, or coal if you feel they deserve it. Notice how it makes you feel. Lighter? Freer? Maybe even a little wicked? That's the joy of reclaiming Christmas — finding small acts of rebellion that remind you the season doesn't have to come gift-wrapped to mean something.

- **Write Your Reclaiming Christmas Pact**
  Write a short, heartfelt promise to yourself about how you'll reclaim Christmas this year. Make it clear, simple, and loaded with permission to let go of perfection. Stick it somewhere visible so when the holiday stress creeps in, you have your reminder: this Christmas is yours.

Take 5 – Checklist

- **Stage a Coal Rebellion**

  Pull an *Adam* and do one thing this Christmas that flips convention on its head.

- **Audit the Magic**

  List the things that genuinely bring you joy — then notice how few of them can be bought. Keep those and let the rest go.

- **Dismantle the Spectacle**

  Unplug from the performance of Christmas — the photos, the matching outfits, the "everything's perfect" routine. Replace it with one moment that's quietly, honestly good.

- **Light the Right Bulb**

  When something (or someone) feels broken, don't just toss it aside. Take the time to fix what matters — the fairy lights, the friendship, the faith in what this day can still be.

- **Channel Your Inner Scrooge (Pre-Ghosts)**

  Say *no* to something ridiculous this season — the overpriced gift, the fifth party, the guilt invite. You don't need three ghosts to show you where your boundaries are.

Quote of Choice

"Christmas isn't a season. It's a feeling." – **Edna Ferber**

(But if that feeling is stress, then it's time to rewrite the script.)

CHAPTER SIXTEEN

Who'll Be Watering Your Roots?

L ast year, amidst the unwashed dishes, a recycled joke about flatulence, and the unmistakable whiff of burnt brandy sauce, I looked around and felt... content.

There was laughter.

There were crumbs.

There were people who love me, even when I'm a hot glue-gun mess of emotion and sarcasm.

And that's when it hit me: they're not here for the photos, the filters, or the performance. They're here because they *see* me. Mess and all.

I had received a Christmas Miracle. While other people were unwrapping socks, scented candles, and soul-sapping disappointment, I unwrapped the most unexpected, utterly delicious gift of all: Mark.

No, he wasn't under the tree (though believe me, I wouldn't mind finding him there in nothing but tinsel). He arrived with something rarer than a Boxing Day refund with no receipt. He showed up fully, heart first, eyes steady, hands warm, and with the kind of emotional intelligence that makes you feel both safe enough to be seen, and bold enough to misbehave.

Let's just say he understands that the best things aren't torn open — they're unwrapped..., slowly..., deliberately..., like a secret you want to savour.

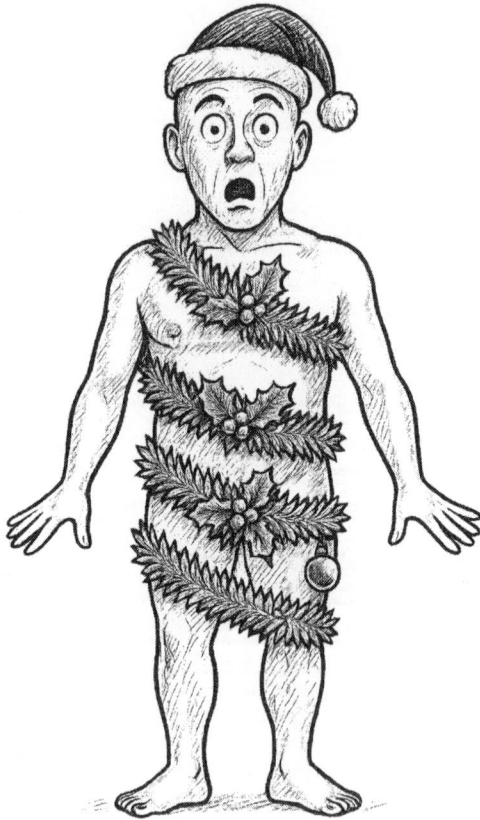

Mark is, quite frankly, exceptional. Not just because he doesn't flinch at the Christmas madness or because he notices when the dishwasher's been emptied (a true holiday miracle), but because he gets me.

The chaos, the mood swings, the glitter in the wine glass-he doesn't just tolerate it; he embraces it, like it's part of the package deal that is *me*. The food on my face, the half-finished projects — he doesn't flinch. He laughs, pours me another glass of wine, kisses my forehead, and smiles. He reminds me that this madness isn't something to fear. And in the middle of the circus – where everyone else might run for cover — he stays.

He stays steady.

He stays kind.

He stays mine.

I feel safe. Not the polite kind of safe, like "text me when you get home," but the bone-deep safe where I can unravel completely. Cry in the kitchen, dance barefoot in the mess of wrapping paper, rant about the unfairness of it all and still know I'm loved. I am safe enough to be ridiculous. Safe enough to be raw. Safe enough to let the mask slip and trust that the person beside me will hold the pieces, not judge them.

That's the real gift right there, isn't it? Not the diamond necklace or the perfectly staged photo, but the person who sees *you* and says, *"I'm not going anywhere."*

Steady. Gentle. Present.

He's not here for the performance (though, honestly — what a performance). He's here for the planting, the growing, and the wildly imperfect, glorious forest that is life with me. He's the one who knows when to hold me steady, when to give me sunlight, and when to quietly water my roots before I even realise I'm wilting.

So let the Christmas chaos come. The turkey can burn, the tree can topple, and a Trump-loving aunt or uncle can bring up politics again — I don't care. Because I know who'll be beside me, watering my roots, laughing, loving, and helping me coax the fairy lights back to life after they short-circuit.

Mark. My Christmas miracle in human form. The greatest *Mark* that has ever been left on me — the one I plan on unwrapping, every damn year.

Lesson Learned: Who'll Be Watering Your Roots?

Congratulations you have graduated.

There is only one more thing to do.

- Look around and notice who's there to water your roots. Maybe it's someone who gives you quiet when you need it, or laughter when you've forgotten what it feels like. Maybe it's the one who hands you a drink, distracts the kids, or simply lets you hide in the bathroom without guilt. If there isn't anyone lucky enough — *yet* — to hold that all-important watering role? Then do it yourself. Water your own roots.

Quote of Choice:

"Christmas shouldn't be about what's under the Christmas tree; it should be about who's watering its roots." – Karie s. Nyarai

CHAPTER SEVENTEEN

Final Thought – Laughing all the way...oh what fun...

S o here we are. Still standing. Slightly glitter-dusted. Emotionally frayed. But together.

Let this be your reminder: You don't have to survive Christmas.

You get to reclaim it. Make it yours. Make it weird. Make it loud, quiet, chaotic, sacred, or pants-optional.

Make it honest. Make it real. Make damn sure it's not about proving anything to anyone.

So, here's to you—rebel of the ribbon-wrapped madness.

Go water your tree. Go water your wine glass. Go water yourself with the kind of love that needs no bow.

You've earned every last drop. And then some.

My New Christmas Rules: The 10 Commandments of Christmas

1. **Thou Shalt Not Apologise** for drinking wine at 10:32 a.m. It's Christmas, not a job interview so get on with it.

2. **Thou Shalt Gift Only the Present** to those who show up physically, emotionally, or spiritually, or with wine. No-shows get socks. Worn previously.

3. **Thou Shalt Honour the Ratio** of decorations: 70% sentimental, 30% "WTF is that?" That's the ratio of joy to chaos we're aiming for.

4. **Thy Pets Are Welcome at the Table.** Passive-aggressive relatives are not. Full stop.

5. **Thou Shalt Not Utter "This is How We Always Do It"** unless thou art actively doing the thing with joy or with gin and you are taking the lead.

6. **Remember the Pantry, and Keep It Holy.** It is a safe space for crying, swearing, inhaling trifle or just taking a quiet moment for yourself.

7. **Thou Shalt Forgive Thyself** for burnt potatoes, and Yorkshire puddings that refuse to rise. They are godless and obey only physics. (As well as for the Sherry you sneaked out the trifle allocation.)

8. **Thou Shalt Snap the Outtakes.** Mid-chaos, mid-laughter, mid-someone-throwing-a-sausage roll. That's the photo worth keeping as well as sharing on social media.

9. **Thou Shalt Not Worship False Perfection.** Instagram is not thy gospel. Reality is. So, stop comparing and just enjoy what is right in front of you.

10. **Thou Shalt Water Thine Own Roots.** If no one else tends to your joy, do it yourself with glitter, gravy, or gin.

Manufactured by Amazon.com.au
Sydney, New South Wales, Australia

30303918R00087